"You need to relax," Mick murmured softly in Cassie's ear.

He noticed that Cassie appeared hypersensitive to their surroundings, her gaze flitting first one direction and then the other, as if expecting the killer to jump out at them.

Pulling her closer, Mick slung an arm around her shoulder, instantly rewarded by Cassie stiffening against him. "Right now you're acting like an FBI agent on the hunt. Remember, that's not our role here. You're a newlywed. Try to look happy."

Cassie looked at him, her blue eyes simmering with emotions he couldn't begin to discern. "Sorry." She drew a deep breath and her body relaxed. Her gaze softened as her lips curled into a smile that instantly fired a ball of heat in the pit of Mick's stomach. "Better?" she asked.

He was almost breathless....

CARLA CASSIDY

SCENE OF THE CRIME: BLACK CREEK

HARLEQUIN®
entertain, enrich, inspire™

Recycling programs
for this product may
not exist in your area.

ISBN-13: 978-0-373-74695-8

SCENE OF THE CRIME: BLACK CREEK

Copyright © 2012 by Carla Bracale

ABOUT THE AUTHOR

Carla Cassidy is an award-winning author who has written more than fifty novels for Harlequin Books. In 1995, she won Best Silhouette Romance from *RT Book Reviews* for *Anything for Danny*. In 1998, she also won a Career Achievement Award for Best Innovative Series from *RT Book Reviews*.

Carla believes the only thing better than curling up with a good book to read is sitting down at the computer with a good story to write. She's looking forward to writing many more books and bringing hours of pleasure to readers.

Books by Carla Cassidy

CAST OF CHARACTERS

Cassie Miller—The lovely FBI agent dislikes three things—chaos, spontaneity and Special Agent Mick McCane—and now she must endure a pretend marriage to him in order to catch a killer.

Mick McCane—He's never forgotten the night of passion he shared with Cassie and now he not only has to play the role of pretend husband to her, but also keep her safe from a serial killer.

Derrick Dark—A member of the founding family of Black Creek and a man with a motive for murder.

Jimbo Majors—A teenager with a simmering rage. Had that rage exploded, resulting in two couples dead in their honeymoon suites?

Sheriff Ed Lambert—Did the lawman long for the good old days and had that yearning become a dark obsession?

Jack Bailey—A homegrown thug with a reputation for violence.

Chapter One

Cassie Miller's low-heeled pumps clicked rhythmically against the tile floor of the hallway that led to her boss's office. For a special agent with the FBI, a summons to Director Forbes's office usually brought with it both an edge of excitement and a faint flutter of dread.

Cassie's excitement far outweighed any dread, for she couldn't imagine anything she'd done that might have gotten her in trouble. In fact, for the nearly year she'd been assigned to the Kansas City, Missouri, field office she'd never come close to being reprimanded. Cassie made it a point to play by the rules.

She was more than ready for a new assignment. It had been months since she'd done anything more than push papers and read through cold case files for a fresh perspective. She was definitely chomping at the bit for some action.

She paused and straightened her white

blouse collar beneath the lightweight navy blue jacket, then self-consciously ran a hand down her pencil-thin navy skirt to make sure it was wrinkle-free. She liked to put her best foot forward when going in front of her boss.

As she began to walk again, her steps faltered slightly. She saw the man approaching the office from the opposite direction. He was clad in tight blue jeans and a navy T-shirt that stretched across his broad shoulders. He carried himself with a loose-hipped gait that instantly spoke of self-confidence and perhaps a touch of arrogance.

There were three things in Cassie's life that she disliked: chaos, spontaneity and the slamming-hot man approaching in her direction, Special Agent Mick McCane.

As he cast her the lazy, sexy grin that danced lightly in the depths of his green eyes and had over half the women in the building in complete lust with him, her stomach muscles kinked into a tight knot.

Please don't be going where I'm going, she thought.

She had spent the past six months of her life trying to avoid being anywhere near Mick. She'd spent the past six months trying to forget the one night when control had slipped away from her and she'd allowed spontaneity a night of freedom.

Her heart clunked to her feet as Mick pulled open the door that led to the director's office. "Afternoon, Cassie." He said her name like it was something exceedingly pleasant on his lips.

"Agent McCane," she replied stiffly. She swept through the door, acutely aware of him following right behind her.

Adrianne Warsaw, the secretary to the director, looked up and smiled. "Ah, good, you're both here. He's waiting for you." She gestured toward the closed door that led to the inner sanctum.

Once again it was Mick who opened the door to usher Cassie inside. She gritted her teeth, smelling his familiar cologne, a spice scent that whispered of something slightly wild and wonderful.

"Agent Miller, Agent McCane." Director Forbes gestured them into the two chairs in front of his massive mahogany desk. "Black Creek, Arkansas," he said when both of them were seated.

Cassie frowned, trying to keep her focus solely on the steel-gray-haired man in front of her instead of the sexy dark-haired man seated far too close to her. "Never heard of it," she replied.

"It's west of Hot Springs, Arkansas, in the Ouachita Mountains. Five years ago it wasn't even a dot on the map, now the mayor is working to have it renamed Honeymoon Haven, the honeymoon capital of this region." Director Forbes leaned forward. "Over the last couple of years the town has exploded with cute little cabins and bed-and-breakfast places, restaurants and shops that cater to the newly wed. It's become a fairly profitable tourist town, and the mayor wants to keep it that way."

"So, what's the problem?" Mick asked. He leaned back in his chair, looking as relaxed as if he were sunning himself on the beach.

"Two honeymooning couples murdered in the last month." Forbes leaned back in his chair, his frown cutting a vertical slash in the center of his broad forehead. "We've been contacted by the local sheriff, Edward Lambert, along with Mayor John Jamison, requesting help with the situation."

A ripple of relief swept through Cassie. It was always easier to work a case when you had the blessings of the locals. Although she didn't want to believe that she'd be working this case with Mick, there was nothing else for her to think with him sitting right next to her and hearing the same information that she was hearing.

"They've managed to keep the murders quiet for the time being, but there's no question that if word of this gets into the media their main source of income from the tourism trade will dry up. Naturally they're both concerned about the murders as well and don't want any more taking place, but because of the similarities of the crime scenes, they don't believe the unsub is finished there."

"Couples murdered…does that mean we're looking at a team of killers?" Mick asked as he sat up straighter in his chair.

"Sheriff Lambert is sure that both couples were murdered by the same person or persons. But at this point it's unclear if we're looking at one or more than one person committing the crimes."

Forbes patted two manila folders in the center of his desk. "I have all of the reports and crime-scene photos here, a copy for each of you. The sheriff faxed me over everything he had on the two cases."

Cassie tried not to think about the victims. Honeymooners, just beginning their lives together. If she allowed herself to think about them in that way then emotions would emerge, and she preferred to remain as objective as possible when working a case. She'd long ago mastered the art of compartmentalization, and it was that skill that made her an efficient and productive agent.

"This killer or killers are particularly nasty pieces of work," Forbes continued. "Each of the couples was killed between eight and midnight while in their cabins. In both cases the men were shot execution style in the back of their heads and the women were gagged and bound on the bed and stabbed to death."

"Sexual assault?" Mick asked, no hint now of his legendary charm in his deep voice.

"Negative," Forbes replied. "Neither woman was sexually assaulted. The coroner report indicates he believes that the men died first and the woman died minutes after, but he admits the timing is so close it could be the other way around."

She felt Mick's gaze on her. Despite her effort to the contrary, Cassie's heart cringed for the victims although she kept her features carefully schooled to show no emotion.

It was obvious she would be working with Mick, and that in and of itself would be a hair-pulling study in frustration, but she would work with the devil himself if it meant stopping a killer.

"Were they killed in the same establishment?" Mick asked.

"No. The first couple was killed at a place called the Wedding Tree Motel. They were staying in unit seven, a secluded little cabin that caters to the needs of a honeymooning couple. They were killed on their fourth night. The second couple had rented a cabin for two weeks at the Bridal Bouquet Honeymoon Cabins. They were murdered on their seventh night there."

"Different time schedules and different locations. Probably a local." Mick frowned thoughtfully as Cassie pulled a small notepad and pen from her pocket.

Mick never took notes. It was one of the things that drove her crazy about him. Within hours of him getting any file of material it would be coffee-stained, probably have pizza sauce dripped on it and the pages would be tossed out of order. Mick McCane was chaos on two long, lean legs.

As Director Forbes shared with them some of the other particulars of the crimes, Cassie took copious notes in the spiral notebook that was as much a part of her wardrobe as her sensible cotton underwear.

On the last case they'd worked together Cassie had asked Mick why he didn't take notes and he'd tapped his temple and stated that all the pertinent information that was needed was carefully stored in his brain. The aggravating part was that he was right. He seemed to have the memory of a computer.

"When do we leave?" Cassie asked, always eager to get away from the quiet, neat apartment where she lived and into the action of a hunt for a killer.

"Tomorrow morning," Daniel Forbes replied. "It's been two weeks since the killer struck, so Sheriff Lambert feels another murder is imminent."

"I'll bet we can find us some amazing moonshine in that part of the country," Mick said. "How does a little firewater sound, Cassie?" Forbes shot him a look of indulgent patience while Cassie gave him a cold, caustic stare.

It hadn't been moonshine that had caused her to completely lose her mind and self-control six months ago. It had been a bottle of Dom Perignon that had made her crazy for

Mick, and she'd never forgive herself for that lapse in judgment.

Because she'd liked it.

She'd liked the wild abandon she'd found in his arms, but he was the last man on earth she'd ever want to be with in any kind of a real relationship. She had a feeling that within a month of spending time with him she'd want to take out her service revolver and shoot him or shoot herself.

"So, I'm assuming the plan is to meet with Sheriff Lambert the minute we hit town," Mick said.

"Actually, Sheriff Lambert and I have agreed to approach this in another way," Forbes replied. "You are to meet the sheriff in a small town called Cobb's Corners about thirty miles outside of Black Creek."

Cassie frowned. "I don't understand." Normally they went in with guns on hips, flashing badges, and dug straight into the investigation.

"Approach things in a different way how?" Mick asked, voicing Cassie's next question.

Director Forbes leaned forward once again, his gaze lingering long and hard on Mick, and then he turned to stare at Cassie. "You two worked quite well together on the Samuel case," he said.

Cassie compressed her lips together to hold back the protest she wanted to voice. No, they hadn't worked well together. Mick had driven her crazy with his laid-back ways, outrageous flirting and disregard for schedules.

Still, she had to admit that when it came to the actual work process their two different styles had melded together well for success.

"In both of these cases," Forbes continued, "the victims appear to be a specific physical type. The men were dark-haired, in good shape, and the women were small in stature and blonde."

Cassie felt a sinking sensation in the middle of her stomach. Surely she was misunderstanding what Forbes had in mind.

"Exactly what is our assignment?" she asked.

"Bait," Forbes replied.

"Bait?" Cassie parroted and slowly turned to look at Mick.

The corners of his sensual lips turned upward as he gazed at her. "Looks like we're going to be newlyweds."

MICK WATCHED THE COLOR BLANCH from Cassie's cheeks, although her pale face remained completely emotionless. She wouldn't show her displeasure at the idea in front of Daniel Forbes. She was too much a professional for that.

Having grown up with three older sisters, Mick had always believed he had a pretty good handle on women, but Cassie Miller had been a mystery from the moment he'd met her seven months before.

She'd come to the Kansas City field office straight from Quantico a year ago and had quickly built a reputation for being intelligent, hard working and a loner.

In the month that Mick had worked with her, he'd found her to be irritatingly obsessive-compulsive, rigid and for some strange reason hotter than hell.

She mystified him like no other woman ever had, and on that night when he'd encouraged her to share a bottle of champagne and they'd wound up in bed, she'd released a passionate wildness that had made him unable to completely forget that night no matter how hard he'd tried.

He refocused his attention on his boss, listening to the plans for the next day. "You will be checking into the Sweetheart Suites tomorrow night as newlyweds Cassie and Mick Crawford. Your new identification and background information is also in the folders. But before that, you are to meet Sheriff Lambert at the Dew Drop Café in Cobb's Corner at two. He'll tell you the rest of the arrangements that have been made for the two of you. This isn't about how well you can investigate the murder. Leave that to the local law enforcement and the other agents I'm sending in. Your job is to strictly play to the victimology of the killer and nothing more. Be a couple of happy honeymooners and let the killer come to you."

Mick hazarded a glance at Cassie, who still looked slightly shell-shocked. He had worked undercover many times, but he was relatively certain that Cassie never had before. There were hazards and tricks she would have to learn, and he wasn't sure she would be a willing student or a quick study. Time would tell.

He once again focused his attention on Forbes, who was finishing up the details of the assignment. "By the time you check in tomorrow afternoon we'll have a surveillance team in place in the cabin next to yours. We're not about to throw the two of you in the path of a killer without a little backup."

"And that's what I like about you," Mick said with his usual humor. Cassie didn't crack a smile. Mick sighed inwardly. He had a feeling this was going to be a brief but difficult marriage.

Once the meeting was finished, he and Cassie stepped out of the office. "This should be interesting," he said.

"I just want you to know that I'm not happy to be working with you again," she said, her bright blue eyes flashing a cold ire. "Working the Samuel case with you was an unpleasant experience I'd rather forget."

"There were moments of it that I'll never forget." He knew they were the wrong words to say the instant they left his mouth.

Her cheeks flushed a bright pink and her blue eyes narrowed slightly. "A momentary lapse of judgment on my part that will never happen again. I'm going home to pack and get ready for this charade. I'll meet you here at seven in the morning."

She didn't give him an opportunity to reply, but rather spun on her heels and hurried down the hallway away from him. He watched her go, his head filled with myriad thoughts. At least she hadn't pretended she didn't remember that night with him.

Of course, it would have been hard to forget the morning after, when she'd shoved him from the bed to the floor and told him to get out of her apartment. "Forget this happened," she'd said. "Forget my address. In fact, forget my name." She'd chased him from the bedroom to the door in a state of barely contained rage.

"Don't forget to pack your bathing suit," he now called after her. Her only response was a visible stiffening of her slender shoulders as she continued on her way.

When she disappeared from the hallway, Mick shook his head ruefully. It was definitely the first time he'd had a reaction like that from a woman he'd had sex with, a woman he'd spent the night with.

Minutes later as he left the field office and drove north toward the house he'd bought a year ago with the intention of renovating, he turned his thoughts to everything that would need to be done before taking off in the morning.

It was already after four. He'd go home, throw some clothing in a duffel bag and then spend the rest of the evening studying the files he'd been given.

There was nothing Mick liked better than hunting killers, and he was good at what he did. Unfortunately, this time he wouldn't be the hunter, and if all things went the way they were supposed to, he and Cassie would be the hunted.

The whole operation was risky. It was possible the killer wouldn't take them as bait, possible that another couple would wind up dead in their place.

The drive to his home took twenty minutes, and by the time he pulled into his driveway he couldn't wait to study the particulars of the crime.

He stifled a mental groan as he pulled up in his driveway alongside his eldest sister's car. At forty-two years old, Lynnette had lost her husband a year ago in a tragic car accident. The two had never had children, and once the initial grieving stage had passed she'd taken to nurturing Mick like she had when they'd been kids.

"Something smells good," he said as he walked through the front door. He headed directly to the kitchen, where he knew he'd find Lynnette.

"Some of my baked ziti and garlic bread." Lynnette turned from the oven and smiled at him. "I fixed too much yesterday and thought I'd bring some of the leftover to you."

He set the folder on the table and sat as she motioned him down in the chair. "Let's see, two days ago you made too much meat loaf. Before that I seem to remember some beef stew magically appearing in my refrigerator."

"What can I say? I like to cook and I always cook too much." She placed a plate in front of him, the scent of her homemade tangy tomato sauce creating a rumble in the pit of his stomach.

"You do realize I'm thirty-four and pretty well grown. You don't have to cook for me," he said, picking up his fork and digging into the tasty pasta dish.

She flashed him her beautiful smile as she sat across from him at the table. "To me you'll always be that five-year-old little charmer that Patsy, Eileen and I worked so hard on to curl your hair and paint your fingernails in an effort to make you our fourth sister."

Mick shot her a mock scathing look and reached for a piece of garlic bread. "You know that experience scarred me for life and was the reason I decided to get one of the most macho jobs on the planet."

Lynnette laughed. "But you did make a really pretty sister." She sobered slightly. "Of course what we'd really like is for you to get married and give us a lovely sister-in-law."

Mick shook his head. "I've told you all

that's not in my plans. I have no interest in ever pursuing love and marriage."

Lynnette leaned back in her chair, her pretty features filled with sadness. "You don't know what you're missing," she said softly.

Mick set down his fork and reached across the table to cover one of her hands with his. "I'm so sorry," he said. They were meaningless words that had been spoken often to Lynnette in the past year.

She nodded. "You can't let one bad experience close off your heart."

He rubbed his thumb across the back of her hand and tried not to think about how devastating he'd found his one real foray into love. "If you had it to do all over again, knowing the outcome, would you still have married Albert?" he asked as he pulled his hand back from hers.

"Absolutely," she replied without hesitation. "A cruel blow of fate took Al away from me far too soon, but nobody can take away my memories of loving and being loved." She cleared her throat and got up from the table. "Now eat before it gets cold," she commanded.

Lynnette hung around long enough to feed Mick and clean up the dishes. "I'm going to be out of town for a little while starting tomorrow morning," Mick said as he walked her to the front door.

"Where are you headed?" she asked.

He smiled teasingly. "Now, you know if I tell you that I'll have to kill you."

"So, it's a new assignment. You will take care of yourself," Lynnette said with concern. "You know the three of us worry about you every time you have to disappear for work."

"And you know what I always tell you, I'm the invincible man with the unbreakable heart," he replied. He kissed her on the cheek and shooed her out the door. "Don't worry, and I'll call you all when I get back in town."

Minutes later, after throwing what clothes he thought he'd need for a "honeymoon," into a large duffel bag, he hunkered down at the kitchen table and began to read through the files that had been prepared for him.

It took him only minutes to become completely immersed in the dark world of murder. The evening hours were eaten up as he studied crime-scene photos and read reports.

One thing he would say about the Arkansas sheriff's department, they'd done a professional job in collecting and processing evidence. The crime-scene photos were clear and captured the horror of the crime. The interviews that had been conducted following each kill appeared to be appropriate.

Midnight came and went, and finally he felt as if he had all the details he needed to walk into the situation. All he had to do to feel confident in this assignment was learn the final elements of the crimes and his and Cassie's role undercover from Sheriff Lambert the next day.

What he wasn't sure of was how prepared Cassie would be to play her part in the charade. There was no question that a part of him anticipated working with her again, that she'd been one of only two women in his life that had been difficult to get out of his mind.

The first woman had professed to love him and then had committed what he considered an unforgivable sin. He would never give a woman that kind of power in his life again.

Unfortunately, he was preparing to go into battle with a woman who he believed wasn't ready for the task ahead, and in this case he wasn't putting his heart on the line, but rather his very life.

Chapter Two

He was late.

Cassie checked her watch for the third time in the past ten minutes. She really wasn't surprised. Mick was the kind of man who would be late for his own funeral.

The last time she'd worked with him his tardiness had definitely been an issue that had driven her half- insane. He'd come in sleepy-eyed and tousle-haired for morning meetings and had often drifted in late to noontime briefings.

Cassie was always early. She considered it the height of rudeness to keep people waiting, but apparently Mick was cut from a different cloth than she'd been.

She impatiently tapped her foot against the pavement of the FBI building parking lot. It already was beginning to heat up beneath the mid-July sunshine.

If they were going to meet with Sheriff

Lambert in Cobb's Corners at two, then they didn't have a lot of time to waste this morning. It was a full six-hour drive to their destination.

The smell of the heating asphalt shot a faint memory through her head, a childhood memory of standing on a hot sidewalk while her parents begged people walking by for spare change.

She shook her head to dispel the painful, shameful memory. She tried never to think of those years of her youth. They brought with them only the tight press of anxiety in her chest and bad dreams at night.

As she checked her watch once again she heard the sound of Mick's little red sports car roaring into the parking lot. A moment later he parked next to her four-door sedan and got out of the driver's seat.

"Good grief, Cassie, you look like you're going to a funeral rather than on a honeymoon," he exclaimed.

Cassie looked down at her casual black slacks and the crisp white short-sleeved blouse she wore and then back at him in his khaki shorts and wildly flower-printed shirt. "Excuse me for not meeting your questionable standards," she said coolly. "I've never been on a honeymoon before."

He grinned at her and then reached into the backseat of his car and withdrew a large duffel bag. "Don't worry about it, when we get to town I'll help you do a little shopping."

She stared at him in horror, her mind instantly filled with a vision of herself in Daisy Duke shorts and see-through blouses. Shopping with Mick McCane? She didn't think so, at least not in this lifetime.

He dropped the duffel next to where she'd parked her medium-size suitcase and smaller overnight bag. "Have you been inside? Do we need to check in or anything?"

"I already did." She held up her left hand that now sported a diamond wedding band.

"Wow, looks like I've got good taste. Wheels?"

She pointed to a nearby navy blue sedan and held up a key. "The paperwork has been done. It's registered to Mick and Cassie Crawford from Kansas City."

"Great, let's load up and hit the road."

They stored their luggage in the trunk and then she slid into the passenger seat as he took the wheel. She was instantly conscious of the scent of his cologne, that spicy scent that evoked memories of twisted sheets and hot kisses and sinful caresses that had driven her out of her mind.

"You've got your new identification?" he asked as they both buckled their seat belts and he backed out of the parking space.

"In my wallet," she replied, thankful that he'd broken the unwanted direction of her thoughts.

"I've got identification and a credit card to use for everything," he said. "I guess we need to come up with a backstory for ourselves." He turned out of the parking lot and onto a street that would eventually carry them out of Kansas City and toward Arkansas.

"If we're on our honeymoon, then I guess we just got married yesterday?"

"Sounds good to me. Most people get married on Sundays, but we decided to have a Monday evening ceremony because we like to be different." He flashed her a quick glance. "Well, if anyone presses the issue we can say *I* like to be different and I pressured you in to a Monday marriage."

"I suppose you want to tell people we met rollerblading on the moon," she said dryly.

He laughed. He had a nice laugh, deep and robust, not that it mattered to her. "Actually, I figured we'd tell people we were introduced by mutual friends."

For the first time since she'd gotten into

the car Cassie began to relax. "Okay, that sounds good. How long did we date before you popped the question?"

"Six months, and then we had a small, intimate ceremony with just friends and family."

"Six months?" She frowned. "That doesn't sound like a very long courtship."

Once again he gifted her with his confident, charming smile. "I know a good thing when I find it, so I didn't waste any time when it came to putting a ring on it."

Cassie started to protest, but instead clamped her mouth firmly closed. What difference did it make what they told anyone who asked? The people in Black Creek were strangers and she and Mick were simply there to do a job. Once that job was done she'd never see any of those people again.

And she had to focus strictly on the work. She couldn't be distracted by the fact that from the moment she'd first met him almost a year ago something about Mick had made her breath catch just a bit in her chest.

"Fine, you moved fast and I fell for your charm," she finally said.

His grin grew downright cheeky. "So, you admit it, you do find me charming."

"Stuff it, McCane," she retorted irritably.

She'd known this was going to be difficult. They were scarcely out of the city limits and already she wanted to jump out of the car and leave him behind.

He seemed to sense that he might have pushed her far enough. He repositioned his hands on the steering wheel and stared out the front window. "The cover story is that I'm a carpenter and work for a big remodeling company and you're a receptionist in a dental office."

"Okay, that sounds fine. Did you read the files?"

"Yeah, I was up most of the night looking at them."

"What were your first impressions?" Cassie asked, even more comfortable as the conversation turned to murder. She didn't want to think about what that said about her social skills or lack thereof.

"Confusing. We know the motive isn't sexual because the women weren't raped or didn't appear to be molested in any way. We also know there was no robbery involved because nothing appeared to be stolen from the rooms or the victims. The men still had their wallets and cash in their pockets and the women still had on their wedding rings. So, right now the motive is up for grabs."

It was always more difficult to solve crimes when the motive wasn't obvious, Cassie thought. "A silencer had to have been used when the men were shot. Otherwise somebody in the area would have heard the gunshot, and according to everything I read nobody in the cabins nearby heard anything."

She smoothed a hand down her slacks, grateful for the cool air that blew through the vents. He was right, she should have dressed even more casually, at least worn a pair of shorts instead of the long slacks.

"What I wasn't able to figure out by reading the reports and looking at the crime-scene photos is who the real victims were in each case. Both husband and wife were killed, but in two different ways, one shot, one stabbed. Which one was the primary target?"

"If we had a motive we might have a better answer to that question. Maybe it's possible they both were the primary targets," she replied. "Hopefully we'll learn more from Sheriff Lambert when we get to Cobb's Corners."

"What I don't get is how the perp managed to get the woman trussed up with duct tape on the bed and control the man at the same time."

He frowned, the gesture doing nothing to detract from his handsome features.

"He had a gun. That's a definite control mechanism."

"Maybe," he conceded. "But you'd think if a man came into your cabin brandishing a gun, somebody would yell or scream and yet the people in the cabins on either side indicated they'd heard nothing when the murders were taking place."

"There was no sign of forced entry into either of the cabins."

"All that means is either the doors were unlocked or they opened the door to the killer. Maybe they knew him, maybe they didn't. Then there's the possibility that it wasn't one man working alone. There's no way to know that at this time." He cast her a quick glance. "Where do you work, Mrs. Crawford?"

"I work for Dr. Davidson, a dentist in Kansas City," she replied without hesitation. "Do you think you need to test me?"

"Just checking."

They fell silent as the wheels of the car continued to thrum against the highway, clipping off the miles that would take them to the small town where four tragic murders had occurred.

Cassie stared out the passenger window, her

thoughts occupied with the files she'd read the night before. Director Forbes had been right. She and Mick fit the profile of the victims to perfection.

Jim Armond and Bill Tanner had both been physically fit, dark-haired young men with sculpted handsome features. There was no question that Mick looked a lot like the two dead men.

Susie Armond and Jennifer Tanner had both been pretty blonde, petite women with blue eyes. They hadn't looked so pretty after having been bound up on the beds and stabbed.

Cassie reached up and touched a strand of her blond hair and then twisted the unfamiliar wedding ring on her finger. There was no question that she could pass for one of the dead women's sisters. She hoped the team that had been assigned to watch Mick and her cabin was on top of its game.

She'd never done anything like this before. She'd never gone undercover and certainly not in a situation where she looked like a potential victim.

She glanced over at Mick. "Have you done this sort of thing before? You know, been undercover?"

"Several times. The longest was for four

months when I went undercover as a home-less man to find a killer targeting that group of people. What about you?"

"No, I've never been undercover," she replied.

"It's like being an actor or an actress. You take on the role of the person you're playing and you eat, sleep and drink it. Are you nervous?"

Cassie hesitated a moment and then finally replied, "Maybe a little bit."

He nodded, as if satisfied with her reply. "You should be. You have to remember that this isn't the case of if you don't play your role right you get fired. This is a role that if you don't do it right you could either get one of us or somebody else killed. You should be nervous. I'm just hoping you're up for this challenge."

"Don't you worry about me. I'm definitely up for the challenge," she replied as a new surge of irritation swept through her. Was he questioning her capabilities? She was a trained agent and she knew exactly what was at stake. The last thing she intended to do was screw things up.

THE CLOSER THEY GOT to Cobb's Corner, the tighter the anxiety in Mick's stomach twisted.

Initially he'd been disappointed when he'd pulled up and he'd seen Cassie standing in the parking lot as if at attention. She'd looked tense and was dressed like she was going off to take notes at a business meeting.

She would have to work a little harder to take on the persona of a young, beautiful bride on her honeymoon. Most people considered their honeymoons one of the happiest times in their marriages. He wouldn't know about that, since he'd never married.

He just hoped she was up to the challenge. And this case was definitely going to be a challenge. They had to consciously attempt to catch the attention of a killer or killers.

Physically they both looked the part, but nobody knew for sure exactly what had drawn the killer to those particular couples besides their outward appearances. Had the couples offended somebody in town? Was it possible their physical appearance was just a coincidence and had nothing to do with why they'd been chosen for death?

So many questions, and he hoped that Sheriff Edward Lambert would be able to give them more clarity on the matter. He also hoped the Dew Drop Café served good food.

They'd made no stops along the way, it was well after noon, and he was starving.

They'd spoken very little on the trip, other than the first flurry of conversation. Cassie appeared to be one of the most self-contained women he'd ever met. Unlike his sisters, she apparently didn't feel the need to fill every silence with idle chatter. He liked that about her.

She was hot and quiet, definitely his kind of woman, but he knew better than to go there again. He couldn't forget the utter contempt she'd shown him after their one night together.

Besides, she possessed other qualities that he knew would make him crazy in a short period of time. He had a feeling she was not only tightly controlled, but also controlling.

Around the office she had the reputation for being Ice Queen material. She didn't have drinks or meals with other agents. In fact, she didn't socialize at all with any coworkers.

She was always up for overtime, indicating she had no social life at all and didn't seem to be looking for a relationship of any kind with any member of the opposite sex despite the fact that he knew she'd just turned thirty years old.

It had been Mick's experience that most women had a little wedding-bell alarm that rang in their heads by their thirtieth birthday, but Cassie didn't appear to be the norm. She didn't seem to possess the desperate "I'm thirty and not married" madness.

"You hungry?" he now asked, breaking the long silence of the trip as they reached the outskirts of the small town of Cobb's Corners.

"Starving," she replied, and then pointed out the window to the left. "There it is."

The Dew Drop Café had a red awning announcing the establishment. It didn't appear too busy at this time of day and Mick pulled into a parking space directly in front.

"I'm not sure what I'm more eager for, information on the crimes or a big juicy cheeseburger," he said as he turned off the car engine.

"I definitely know what I'm eager for. Information that will let us get this job done quickly and successfully." She opened her car door and got out.

Mick did the same, the humid July heat slapping him in the face like a spurned lover. He was grateful for the dorky tourist shirt he wore. At least it was lightweight and breathed.

The Dew Drop Café was less charming inside than it had looked on the outside. The interior paint was old and peeling, the red bar stools sported rips, and the red vinyl booths also showed signs of wear and tear. Even though there were half a dozen people inside it was easy to spot Sheriff Edward Lambert, despite the fact that he wasn't in uniform.

The older man, with a shock of white hair, sat at the back of the restaurant facing the door, intelligent brown eyes taking in everything and everyone in the room. Those eyes widened slightly as he caught sight of Mick and Cassie.

They approached his table, introductions were made, orders were taken by a waitress and then Cassie excused herself for the restroom.

"Ambience stinks but the food is great," he said.

"That's good to know," Mick replied.

"I wanted to meet you two here instead of someplace in Black Creek so that we can keep this whole operation under wraps," Lambert said as he wrapped big hands around the coffee mug in front of him. "Even though we're a tourist trap and are still fighting over what the name of the town is eventually going to be, we're also a small town where secrets are sometimes hard to keep. This whole thing won't work if word gets out that the two of you are FBI agents."

Mick nodded. "I completely agree." The two men small-talked about the drive and the hot weather and by that time Cassie returned to the table.

"There's no question that the two of you make the perfect bait physically," Lambert said.

"Have you figured out if the killer's trigger is something more than physical appearance?" Cassie asked as she reached out to align the salt and pepper shakers next to each other in the center of the table.

"Nothing so far. What we have learned is that the two couples pretty much followed the same kind of schedules while they were in town. I've got a list of places they visited and activities they did. I'll give you each a copy before we leave here."

"I read in the file that Jim Armond was an insurance salesman from Oklahoma, and Bill Tanner was a mechanic from Missouri. Any indication that the couples knew each other?" Cassie asked.

"None," Sheriff Lambert replied. "At least none that we've been able to find so far. I've got a six-man force, all good men who have been working overtime to figure this out." He stopped talking as the waitress appeared with their orders.

The decor inside the café might be questionable, but Mick eyed the thick cheeseburger and order of fries in front of him with appreciation. Cassie had ordered a salad, dressing on the side and Ed Lambert had ordered a piece of pie to go along with his coffee.

"I've got to admit that I'm understaffed and pretty much over my head with these murders," the sheriff continued as the waitress moved away from the table. "I've been understaffed for the last couple of years as the town has gained more of a reputation as a hot spot for honeymooning couples." He frowned. "When Mayor John Jamison got his bright idea about this Honeymoon Haven nonsense he turned our quaint little town into a mess."

He paused and took a sip of his coffee. "There's plenty of money flying around town, but none of it has allowed me to hire on more deputies and the petty crime rate has tripled."

"Sounds tough," Mick said.

The older man shrugged. "We do the best we can, but I want to assure you these murders are on the top of our priority list. Unfortunately, they aren't the only things we can focus on with all my manpower. Your boss has assigned another couple to help with the investigation. They'll be staying at the Super Eight Motel just north of town. Director Forbes indicated they would be your contact if you stumble across any information that might be useful."

"Their names?" Mick asked.

"Agents Rick Burgess and David Ellsworth. They'll be working with me and my team, but flying under the radar. The mayor is insistent that we keep this all as low-key as possible. Needless to say, we're not eager for any publicity concerning the murders."

Mick nodded. He was glad to know there were two agents working with the sheriff. He knew both agents, had worked cases with them before and trusted them. He had cell phone numbers for both of them and would check in with them once he and Cassie got settled in town.

"Your tech support team arrived this morning," Ed continued. "Three men checked into the cabin next to yours. They let me know that they had their audio in place and were ready for your arrival."

"Audio?" Cassie looked from the sheriff to Mick, who shrugged.

"According to the agent I spoke to early this

morning they have placed listening devices in the room where you'll be staying. They'll be able to hear anything that happens, but also told me to let you know they didn't bug the bathroom."

Mick smiled at Cassie. "That means if you decide to verbally abuse me it will be all over headquarters before the day is over."

"I have no intention of verbally abusing you," she replied with a flash of her brilliant blue eyes. "Unless you need it," she added under her breath.

Sheriff Lambert cleared his throat. "The good news is that if somehow, someway, the killer gets into your premises, your agents will hear everything that is going on and can get inside within seconds."

Cassie's eyes turned somber and Mick wondered if she'd really considered how badly this assignment could go. They were intentionally putting themselves in the direct path of a killer or killers. If the killer did manage to get into their room it would only take him seconds to shoot Mick and stab Cassie.

What Mick had no intention of telling her was that while he was being hunted, he intended to do a little hunting of his own. Although their job was merely to act the part of newlyweds, to draw the attention of the killer and allow their support team to make an arrest, Mick would investigate independently to find the killer. Even knowing Burgess and Ellsworth were assigned to the case wouldn't stop him from working on his own.

He wasn't about to get trapped in a honeymoon cabin with a killer and depend on a team to rescue him. He'd find the killer long before the game went on that long.

He'd only been blindsided once in his life, and that had been by a woman with blue eyes and a dark soul. He'd never let a woman close to him again, and he wasn't about to allow a killer to get the upper hand on him either.

Chapter Three

It was just after three-thirty when Mick and Cassie were back in the car and headed toward Black Creek, aka Honeymoon Haven.

Cassie pulled out the list of the places the murdered honeymooning couples had visited before their deaths and stared at it in horror. Drinks by the pool, hot springs treatments at the local spa, candlelight dinners and a romantic canoe trip down Black River, and throughout it all she would have to pretend that she was madly, desperately in love with her husband, Mick. If she could pull this off, she'd deserve an Academy Award.

She cast him a surreptitious glance. He appeared to be so relaxed, as if they were taking a vacation rather than putting their lives on the line to catch a killer.

There was a part of Cassie that wasn't afraid of death, times when she woke up in the middle of the night vaguely surprised that she had managed to survive the madness of her childhood.

No, she wasn't afraid of dying, but she *was* afraid of not doing her job properly, of somehow screwing up and letting a killer continue his work or getting somebody else killed by her carelessness.

Gazing out the window, she noticed the road they traveled was narrow and winding through the Arkansas hilly landscape. The scenery was breathtaking. Tall trees crowded the sides of the roads while woods parted occasionally to show a glimpse of bubbling streams sparkling in the bright sunshine.

She knew what she'd signed up for, she knew they were headed to a place called the Sweetheart Suites where there would be one big bed for them both to share, one small space for them both to maneuver.

Still, the closer they got to Black Creek the more real everything became for her. She hadn't shared a bed with a man for any reason in a while. The last time had been eight years ago when she'd been dating Glen Morrow.

Glen had been a nice man, but by the end of the relationship things had gotten strained between them. Glen had finally broken it off, telling her that she had too many control issues for him to handle, that she made it impossible for anyone to love her.

Cassie had been secretly relieved. The sex had been okay, the companionship had been nice most of the time, but she hadn't been in love with Glen and she certainly hadn't been looking for marriage or children. She knew her limitations and she knew that inviting people into her life brought the kind of chaos she didn't want or need.

She glanced over at Mick. At least she didn't have to worry that a pretend honeymoon would make her fall crazy in love with him. She recognized on a base level that he threatened everything she'd worked so hard to maintain, that inviting him into her life in any way would be the biggest mistake she'd ever make.

As they crested a hill the small town of Black Creek appeared in the valley below, and as they drew closer it was obvious that honeymoon madness had possessed what had once probably been a quaint little place.

The road they were on went right through the main business district, with shops and restaurants on either side. The Wedding Cake Café, Bride and Groom Boutique, Newlywed Night Shop for Adults, all the storefronts looked as if a pink and red and white froth had exploded all over the buildings.

Interspersed amid the honeymoon-themed businesses were others that indicated the mayor hadn't been completely successful yet in the formal renaming of Black Creek to Honeymoon Haven. The Black Creek Bank rose up three stories, stately and gray next to the Black Creek Grocery Store.

Mick turned into an entrance that led to the Sweetheart Suites and parked in front of the building marked as the office. As he got out of the car to go inside and get the key to their unit, Cassie looked around the general area.

Tiny mauve-colored cabins were nestled amid tall, fully leaved trees, and on the opposite side of the office was a swimming pool complete with a grotto and a waterfall.

An edge of anxiety pressed against her chest and she turned to look in the opposite direction. Cassie liked water only if it was contained in a bathtub.

For a brief moment she was thrown back in time and the water surrounded her as she flailed helplessly, going under the surface as her lungs threatened to burst. She reached the surface. The only sound she heard was her own frantic gasps for breath and her parents' crazy laughter before the water pulled her down once again.

She now pulled in a deep breath of the fresh-scented air, sat up straighter in her seat and shook off the memory as Mick returned to the car.

"Lucky number seven," he said and handed her the key on a heart-shaped key ring.

"This whole town feels kind of cheesy, don't you think? All the hearts and flowers and lace kind of make me want to gag," she said.

"Cassie, where's your sense of romantic spirit?" he asked as he put the car into gear and headed to their cabin. "I think it's kind of charming."

She looked at him in surprise. "I'd never guess you for a romantic kind of guy."

He smiled. "Actually, I love romance, I just don't want it to mislead any woman into thinking I want anything to do with marriage."

"We're definitely on the same page there," Cassie replied. "I never want to get married."

"Never say never," Mick replied, parking the car in front of their little cottage. "Home, sweet home, let's grab the bags and check things out."

Imagining a honeymoon cottage and actually being in one were two very different things, Cassie thought as the two of them entered unit seven.

It was one large room, with a king-size bed resting on a platform that made it the focal point. The bedspread looked as it had been made by a thousand lace doilies sewn together. Scattered across the top of the white lace were delicate pink rose petals.

A dresser with a flat-screen television on top sat at the end of the bed with a chair next to it. The only other furniture in the room was a love seat behind a coffee table that sported a fruit-and-muffin basket obviously intended as a continental breakfast and a bottle of champagne chilling on ice in a silver-plated bucket.

Cassie dropped her suitcases on the floor and walked over to the bathroom. She gasped as she peered inside, where a Jacuzzi tub big enough for four people sat in the center of the room. The glass-enclosed small shower, sink and stool seemed to be incidental.

"Definitely not the average motel room," Mick said from over her shoulder.

It was Cassie's nightmare. The room breathed of intimacy, of items and furniture placed specifically to promote sexuality and love. She was grateful when Mick stepped back from her and walked to the love seat.

He sank down and pulled out the paperwork that Sheriff Lambert had given them. He spread out the pieces of paper on the table before him.

"According to this information the three agents next door are Sam Hunter, Jacob Tyler and Bob Hastings." He looked around the room. "Let's see if they're ready for us. Agent Hastings, if you can hear me, please walk outside your cabin door and let me see you."

Together, Cassie and Mick peered out their front window to the cabin next door. The door opened and a tall blond man walked outside. He stretched with arms overhead and gave a small but perceptible nod of his head, then returned back inside his cabin.

"Okay, so we're wired for sound," Mick said as they both moved away from the window. "I suppose our next order of business is to get unpacked and figure out what we're going to do with what's left of the day."

"I never unpack when I travel," she said. "I prefer just living out of my suitcases."

He gazed at her curiously. "Funny, I would have definitely pegged you for the kind of woman who has to iron and hang everything the minute you check in someplace."

"That just goes to show you how little you

know about me," she replied. There had been far too many times in her childhood that she'd been roused in the middle of the night to run from some motel or rented room with only the clothes on her back, leaving everything she owned behind because they weren't in a suitcase she could carry out. But she wasn't about to share the madness of her childhood with anyone, especially Mick.

"Well, I'd better get my shirts hung up, otherwise everyone will wonder why you married such a wrinkled man." As he began to hang his shirts in the closet just off the bathroom, Cassie thought about the clothes she had packed.

Her entire wardrobe consisted of clothing that didn't need to be ironed, that could be pulled from a suitcase and put right on. She sank down on the love seat. She didn't want to think about clothes.

She also didn't want to think about sharing that big bed with Mick, surrounded by his scent, warmed by his body heat. There was no way she wanted to go there again.

What she wanted to focus on most of all was what came next in their quest of catching the eye of a killer and hopefully getting him off the streets before he killed again.

It would be nice if they'd gain his attention today and he'd try to strike at them tonight, before she had to climb into that bed with Mick.

"I THINK OUR FIRST order of business is to take a little stroll down Main Street," Mick said once he'd hung his shirts and shorts in the closet. "A fish has to see the bait before he'll bite on it." He checked his watch. "We can take a stroll, visit a couple of shops and then end up having a nice intimate dinner at the Love Nest Fine Dining Restaurant."

"Somehow it's difficult for me to imagine love nest and fine dining in the same sentence," she said dryly.

Mick laughed and grabbed her by the elbow. "Come on, my lovely new bride. It's time to get to work."

He felt the tension that radiated from her at his simple touch. As they left the cabin he released his hold on her elbow and instead grabbed her hand with his. "You're going to have to do better than that, cupcake," he said beneath his breath as he squeezed her cold, lifeless hand.

Her cheeks grew pink and she returned his squeeze. He knew this all was going to be difficult on her. She obviously hated him. It was like she blamed him for somehow taking advantage of her the night they'd fallen into bed together.

He wasn't about to take on that responsibility. She might protest that she'd been drunk, but the bottle of wine had been small and she hadn't appeared inebriated in any sense of the word. It had been mutual desire, not booze, that had driven them into bed together.

As they left the Sweetheart Suites grounds and hit the main drag, they joined a throng of couples wandering the street and drifting in and out of shops. Laughter filled the air and everywhere Mick looked there were public displays of affection.

As they walked he glanced in the shopwindows they passed, not looking inside the stores themselves but rather eyeing their reflection in the glass to see if anyone in particular followed them.

It was probably too soon for that, but he did wonder if one of the agents from the cabin next to theirs would be shadowing their movements. He hoped not—a stranger walking the streets alone in this town of couples would possibly draw some attention and might scare off the person they wanted to follow them.

He consoled himself with the fact that neither of the murdered couples had been killed outside of their rooms, so he seriously doubted they had an FBI shadow. They would be closely monitored when in their cabin, but there was no reason to believe that any danger would come at them on the streets.

He noticed that Cassie appeared hypersensitive to their surroundings, her gaze flitting first one direction and then the other, as if expecting the killer to jump out at them.

Pulling her closer, he slung an arm around her shoulder, instantly rewarded by her stiffening against him. "You need to relax," he murmured softly in her ear. "Right now you're acting like an FBI agent on the hunt. Remember, that's not our role here. You're a newlywed. Try to look happy."

She looked at him, her blue eyes simmering with emotions he couldn't begin to discern. "Sorry." She drew a deep breath and her body next to his relaxed. Her gaze softened as her lips curled into a smile that instantly fired a ball of heat in the pit of his stomach. "Better?" she asked.

He was almost breathless. He nodded and got them walking again. For the next few minutes they nodded and greeted other couples they passed as Mick kept his attention off Cassie and instead got the lay of the land.

The center of town was basically three blocks long, with side streets sporting signs pointing to other charming shops and eateries catering specifically to newlyweds that were located off the main drag.

On the surface the town appeared to have already made the transition from Black Creek to Honeymoon Haven, but there were definitely signs of a town divided.

The bank and the grocery store weren't the only buildings that still held their Black Creek identity with the town name plastered across the front of their buildings. The post office, a Chinese restaurant and a dress boutique all still held the Black Creek name.

Flyers stuck to street signs they passed protested the new name and asked for the mayor's resignation. "Looks like trouble in paradise," Cassie said apparently observing the same things he had along the way.

"Mayor Jamison definitely appears to have his hands full," Mick agreed. He pointed just ahead and on the opposite side of the street where a storefront at the very end of the block was plastered in the same flyers and large signs that read Stop the Madness.

"Looks like a place we should check out," Cassie said as she moved from beneath his arm. He was surprised to realize that he'd enjoyed the warmth of her curves against him and the clean, slightly floral scent that emanated from her.

He followed just behind Cassie as they crossed the street, unable to help but notice the slight sway of her hips beneath the tailored slacks. It was obvious she was much more relaxed without any physical contact between them. That was definitely going to have to change.

He hurried to catch up with her as they reached the building. The doors were locked, but a sign indicated that it was the headquarters of an organization fighting the name change of the city.

A metal rack just outside the front door held flyers and Mick picked one up, folded it up and tucked it in his back pocket to look at more closely later.

"How about we find that restaurant and grab some dinner." Cassie nodded her agreement and they started back the way they'd come, seeking the Love Nest Fine Dining, a place where both of the murdered couples had enjoyed a meal.

He once again took Cassie's hand in his as they walked. She was still tense, as if she didn't like the feel of his skin against hers.

He shot her a quick glance and she looked neither happy nor honeymoon-like. He released a deep sigh. "Am I going to have to remind you all the time that we're on stage here, that you have to play your role at all times? I know you don't like me, but you've got to suck it up and pretend otherwise."

She sidled closer to him. "I've just been focusing on everything and everyone around us."

"I told you that's not our job. We need to give the impression that we're focused only on each other. Remember, we just got married and can hardly keep our hands off each other. We don't want to screw up this assignment because of personal issues."

"I don't have any personal issues with you," she protested.

He narrowed his eyes and looked at her in disbelief. "Is that your final answer?"

"If I say yes do I win a chance at the speed round?"

He smiled. "Nah, I just get the satisfaction of knowing we don't have any dramatic baggage lingering between us."

They stopped at the door of the restaurant and Mick looked at her expectantly, surprised to realize he wanted an answer from her. He wanted to know why she'd been so cold toward him after the night they'd shared together, why she'd acted so violently after they'd made love. He'd thought about it far too often in the months since it had happened.

Her gaze skittered away from his. "That night was a mistake, Mick. I just don't like to mix business with pleasure," she finally answered. She looked back at him, a touch of steely strength in her eyes. "Now, let's leave it at that and get on with our assignment."

He wasn't really satisfied with her reply, but recognized that she had no intention of talking about it any further.

The Love Nest Fine Dining Restaurant was comprised of semicircular booths covered on the outside with a faux strawlike material that gave them the impression of nests.

Mick requested seating by the front window and they were led to one of the "nests" where they could be seen by people out on the street while they enjoyed their meal.

It took only a few minutes for them to order a glass of wine and then select their meal from the menu, which offered meals for two to share.

When the waitress left, Cassie leaned toward Mick. "Did you notice anyone suspicious? Anyone paying special attention to us?"

He couldn't help but smile at the eagerness that lit her eyes. Only somebody like him could get excited about catching the attention of a killer.

"I didn't notice anyone."

"I don't think we have a tail," she replied. "I guess since the murders were accomplished in the cottages where the couples were staying they decided not to put a tail on us when we're out in public."

"That's the same conclusion I came to," he replied.

"If the first two murders were about two weeks apart, then our killer should be ready to pop off again." She paused as the waitress arrived at the table with their drinks.

"Tell me, Cassie, what made you choose to become an agent?" he asked once the waitress had gone. In the time they'd spent together working previously they'd never really had a chance to talk about their personal lives.

They'd worked the case hard and then had celebrated with the fall into her bed. She'd then kicked him to the curb and there had been no time for really getting to know each other. He figured this was as good a time as any to find out more about her. Maybe sharing a little bit between them would loosen her up a bit.

She neatly aligned her silverware next to her plate before looking at him and replying. "Unlike a lot of people who enter law enforcement, I didn't have any family members who worked in the field and none of my family had ever been victims of a violent crime. It was the discipline that drew me, the knowledge that there were definitive rules to adhere to and set procedures to follow. I like that in life. I like structure, both in my professional and in my private life."

"I kind of figured that out about you," he replied dryly.

"What about you?" She reached out and grabbed the stem of her wineglass. He noticed that her fingernails were short and neat and appeared to be painted with clear polish.

She was definitely low maintenance when it came to personal appearance, so unlike the woman who had stolen his heart and then shattered it years ago.

He shoved away thoughts of Sarah. She had

no place in his thoughts anymore. She didn't deserve to be in his thoughts at all.

"Actually, I joined the academy to escape three older sisters who, when I was young, tried to transform me into another sister and now all think they are my mother."

She smiled, a quick gesture that lasted only a moment. "Your mother is gone?" she asked.

He nodded. "A long time ago. She died of cancer when I was seven. My dad worked hard to take care of things, but the maternal stuff all came from my sisters. Dad passed away three years ago from a heart attack and since then my sisters have all stepped up their mothering of me. What about you? You have family somewhere?"

"None," she replied without hesitation. "What do you think about our unsub? Maybe his parents got a divorce when he was young and he blames them for ruining his life so now he's killing newlywed couples before they can become Mommy and Daddy and screw up another kid's world."

Mick didn't miss how smoothly she'd deflected the conversation away from anything personal about herself and back to a professional topic. "Maybe, who knows? Maybe he just likes what he does and we'll never know a motive that makes any kind of sense to any-one. Maybe he just does it for the thrill of it."

She frowned thoughtfully. "Those are the hardest kind of killers to catch, but I don't think that's what we're looking at here. The fact that he's already established a pattern in his victimology tells me there's a reason for the murders, and we just need to crawl into his head to find it."

"It's not our job to get into his head," Mick reminded her. "Our job is to hope that he gets us into his head and sees us as his next vic-tims."

"There's no question that we're his type. I just hope that there are a lot of brunette women on the streets over the next couple of days. That would definitely make it easier for him to spot me. I want him to make his move on us as quickly as possible."

Mick reached across the table and covered her hand with his. "Trying to get rid of me so fast?" He didn't wait for her reply. "Just remember that the better we play our parts the faster we'll make it happen and then you won't have to pretend that you're in love with me any longer."

The conversation was interrupted by the ar-rival of the waitress with their food. While they ate they kept the conversation neutral, mostly talking about the sights they'd seen earlier while strolling down the streets. Several times Mick tried to learn a little about her past, about her parents and where she'd come from, but she deftly managed to respond to his questions without giving him any real answers.

There was a mystery in the depths of her eyes. He sensed secrets in her past, and as far as Mick was concerned there was nothing so inviting as a woman with many layers.

The next couple of days or so should be very interesting, he thought as he eyed Cassie across the table. He wanted to learn a little more about her, unpeel some of the layers to expose the woman beneath the efficient, anal-retentive agent, and if that wasn't enough, he had a killer to bring down.

HE WATCHED THEM from across the street, the dark-haired man and the petite blonde eating dinner at a table near the window of the restaurant.

They were perfect.

They were just what he liked.

And they were FBI agents.

By now, Matt and Janice Campbell, who

ran the Sweetheart Suites, would have told half a dozen friends all about the three agents who had checked into the suite next to Mr. and Mrs. Crawford and the audio equipment they'd installed in that cabin. Of course, Matt and Janice would have sworn each and every person they told to secrecy, but there weren't many secrets in Black Creek.

Three FBI agents holed up in a cottage and two more pretending to be newlyweds, and they all were here because of him.

To catch him.

A thrill swept through him, warming his heart, which had been cold for a long time. FBI agent or not, the woman definitely stirred him. She appeared so fragile, so dainty and small of stature. He could imagine the silky feel of her pale blond hair entwined with his fingers, imagine the horror of her blue eyes as she realized she was about to die.

The very sight of her whirled a rage through him that had been born two years ago and had only been sated twice since then, and that had been when he'd killed those other two couples.

Clenching his hands into fists at his sides he watched as she picked up her wineglass and took a sip. It tickled him that he knew they were playing a part specifically to trap him.

He was sure they'd studied all the facts of the other murders, memorized each and every detail of his handiwork. But he'd been good. He'd been very good. He'd left nothing behind to identify him, no trail for them to follow.

And now they thought they were one step ahead of him, dangling the perfect bait right before his hungry eyes. Yes, that definitely amused him.

He knew they were expecting him to strike in their room, just like he'd taken down the others. They would believe that when danger came it would appear at their cottage door late in the evening.

They would anticipate that he'd established a pattern and would continue to repeat that pattern. That's why they were here. That's why there were three agents in the cottage next to theirs, to wait for him to take their bait, to watch for him to make his move.

He turned and headed down the street, leaving the two to their "romantic" meal. What they didn't know was that he was on to them.

They had no clue that all of their preparations, all their anticipation of his next move was for nothing. Oh, yes, he was on to them and all that meant was that it was time to change his pattern so he could take them down.

The fact that they were FBI agents didn't matter. What did matter was they were a perfect couple...that she was the perfect woman to take away his rage...at least for a little while.

Chapter Four

Cassie awoke just before dawn, superaware of Mick in the bed next to her. The scent of his spicy cologne lingered faintly in the air and even though he was several inches away from her she imagined she could feel the warmth of his body radiating outward to embrace her.

She'd been awake for most of the night, afraid that somehow in her sleep she'd roll over against Mick or worse, snuggle against him while dreaming.

She'd known it would be awkward and it had been, at least for her. Thankfully, when they'd returned to the cabin after dinner she'd gone directly into the bathroom, where she'd changed into a pair of navy blue short-sleeved cotton pajamas, and when she'd come out Mick had already been in bed wearing a T-shirt and a pair of boxers.

She'd slid beneath the sheets on her side of the bed and had held her breath. She had no idea what to expect from him, was afraid that he might try a repeat of what they had shared months ago.

Instead he'd murmured a good-night and within minutes his light snores had filled the air and Cassie had tried her best to relax.

But "relax" didn't seem to be in her body's repertoire of tricks, and sleep seemed out of the question altogether. The day's events played and replayed in her mind. Had the killer already seen them? Was he at this very moment deciding the right time to somehow attempt to gain entry into their room and commit murder once again?

She knew the door was locked and both she and Mick had their service revolvers on the nightstands on either side of the bed. If somebody came through the door they'd be faced with the business end of two guns and the additional support of the three agents in the next cottage.

Then there was the issue of the physical contact with Mick throughout the afternoon and evening. It had been difficult. Each touch of his hand had evoked memories of what they'd shared that single night six months before.

She didn't want to think about that night,

when for a brief moment in his arms she'd finally felt at home, that she was where she belonged. It had been a feeling meant to fool her, to beckon her to let down her guard. And that would be a huge mistake.

It had taken her years to recover from the chaos of her childhood. She now lived her life by her terms, and those terms had already chased one man away from her. She had no intention of attempting anything with any other man. It would simply be a heartbreaking mess, and Cassie hated messes.

Even now, knowing that Mick's shorts and flowered shirt were in a pile at the end of the bed, made her just a little crazy. She'd asked him before he'd fallen asleep what the plans were for today and he'd told her they'd play it by ear.

Play it by ear. She didn't like to work that way. She wanted specific plans, a timeline of how the day's events would unfold. She liked schedules and spreadsheets, and she had a feeling both were totally alien to Mick.

He would be the worst person in the world to fall in love with, and that's why it was dangerous for her to remember that night, those moments when she'd felt so right in his big, strong arms.

Knowing that any more sleep would be impossible, she slid from the bed and padded into the bathroom for a quick shower. The brisk spray helped to slough off any drowsiness that might remain from her nearly sleepless night. She had to be alert, on top of her game today.

At least she hadn't had one of her nightmares, the ones that woke her up weeping. That would have been beyond embarrassing. It would have made her look weak, and that was unacceptable. She'd been weak as a child but she would never be weak again.

Remembering the heat from the day before, she dressed in a pair of tailored navy shorts and a light blue short-sleeved button-up blouse. As she opened the bathroom door the scent of freshly brewed coffee filled her nose.

Mick was up, still clad in his boxers and T-shirt, rich, dark, slightly curly hair tousled from sleep and a lazy smile on his lips as he gestured toward the coffeemaker on the dresser. "Good morning."

"Good morning," she returned, trying not to notice how utterly hot he looked fresh out of the sheets. It should be against the law for a man to look like he did at this very moment.

"Coffee is made. Enjoy a cup while I shower and then we'll talk about the day." He disappeared into the bathroom and Cassie reminded herself to breathe.

She poured herself a cup of coffee and carried it to the front window. Would today be the day that they caught the killer's eyes? She took a sip of the warm brew in an effort to banish the chill that seeped through her body at the thought.

Yet wasn't that exactly what she wanted? The sooner they caught the killer's attention, the faster this assignment would be over and she and Mick would once again go their separate ways.

It had been two weeks between the two murders, so if the killer was on that kind of time line, then he should be ready to kill again at any time.

The rising sun shot splendid colors across the eastern skies and for a moment she was caught up in the beauty before her. She imagined that Black Creek had been a picturesque little town before the honeymoon madness had taken over.

She turned away from the window, remembering the Stop the Madness storefront they'd seen the day before. She certainly didn't have to look far for the shorts Mick had worn the night before. They were still on the floor next to the bed.

She set her cup on the coffee table and walked over to Mick's shorts and plucked them off the floor. She grabbed the flyer he'd stuck in his pocket, then neatly folded both shorts and shirt. She laid them on the dresser next to the flat-screen television and quickly made up the bed.

A few minutes later she unfolded the flyer and sat on the love seat to read what it was all about. She'd just finished looking it over when Mick came out of the bathroom on a breeze of steam and with the scent of clean male, shaving cream and a whisper of spicy cologne.

His denim shorts showcased the slim but strong length of his legs and the short-sleeved chambray shirt exposed his amazing biceps and emphasized his broad shoulders. He glanced at the bed and then at her. "You know the maid would have done that."

"I know, I just don't like to look at an unmade bed."

"Interesting reading?" he asked as he walked over to the coffeemaker and poured himself a cup of the brew.

"These people are definitely resisting changing the name of the town," she said, far too conscious of him as he sank down next to her on the love seat, which seemed to shrink with his presence. "And guess who the president of the movement against the name change is? Derrick Black, great-great-grandson of the founder of the town."

He raised one of his eyebrows and took a sip of his coffee. "Sounds like somebody we should meet," he said as he set his cup down close to hers on the table. He grabbed one of the fat muffins from the basket and unwrapped it. "Eat up, we shouldn't be seen outside before nine or ten this morning."

"Why not?" she asked curiously. It was only a little after seven now. Why not get a jump on the day? "Haven't you heard the old adage about early birds and worms?"

Once again one of his dark eyebrows rose as a provocative grin curved his lips. "We're newlyweds, Cassie. We'd linger in bed, maybe share a little morning delight before heading out to see the sights." He set the muffin down. "Want to share a little morning delight with me, Cassie?"

"Don't be ridiculous," she replied, and then blushed as she remembered that there were extra ears in the room, that the agents in the next cottage could hear whatever they were saying.

Mick laughed good-naturedly. "Have a muffin and relax," he said. He leaned closer to her. "But sooner or later we're going to talk about what happened six months ago," he whispered.

"There's nothing to talk about," she whispered back. "And now the subject is closed."

For a long moment his green eyes held hers, and in their depths she saw questions, questions that she had no intention of ever answering. She broke the eye contact, picked up her coffee cup and got up from the love seat.

She didn't look at him until she reached the window. "So what are the plans for the day?"

He picked up his muffin and took a bite and shrugged. "I figured we'd just kind of hang loose and see what sounds good. We've got a list of places where the murdered couples went and we need to work in one or two of those."

A familiar edge of anxiety fired off in Cassie's brain. "I'd rather we have a more definitive plan for the day. What time do you plan for us to leave here this morning and what, specifically, do we have on our agenda?"

He looked at her as if she were a creature from outer space, the same way Glen had looked at her at the very end of their relationship. It made her feel abnormal, as if there was something wrong with her.

"I'd forgotten that about you," he finally said. He took another bite of his muffin and chewed, his gaze thoughtful as it lingered on her. "Is this some kind of weird control issue that you have?"

"Of course not," she scoffed, and smoothed her hands down the sides of her shorts. "I just like to know how to mentally prepare for the day," she countered.

"Why do you need to mentally prepare for a day of hanging out in a honeymoon town?"

"I just do, okay? So can you humor me in this and give me some specifics?" She tried desperately to keep the anxiety out of her voice.

He popped the last of the muffin in his mouth and followed it by a drink of coffee before replying. "Okay, we'll leave here around nine and the first thing on our agenda will be a visit to the local spa. A little soak and relaxation sounds like the perfect way to start the day. After that I'd like to check out the Stop the Madness headquarters, and by that time it should be lunch."

She nodded, the knot of anxiety in her chest slowly ebbing away. "And after lunch?"

Mick pulled from the paperwork on the table the list of activities the murdered couples had done before they'd been killed. "We can either lounge around by the pool or visit a couple of the shops that are on this list. By then it will be dinnertime at the Wedded Bliss Buffet and Grill."

"Thank you," she said as the last of her anxieties vanished.

"Do we need to do this each morning?"

"It would make me feel better," she admitted.

"Okay then. Now why don't you tell me about what you read in that flyer?"

For the next thirty minutes they talked about what they'd learned so far about the small town of Black Creek aka Honeymoon Haven.

Cassie ate one of the muffins and then peeled an orange as they dissected the original murders and speculated on how long it would take for them to gain the killer's attention.

At a few minutes before nine she grabbed a tote bag she'd carried in her suitcase and placed a bathing suit and a hairbrush inside it. She'd bought the turquoise one-piece bathing suit the evening of the day she'd discovered she was coming here.

Since she hated the water, she didn't swim and hadn't owned a suit. When she went to the store her intention had been to buy a basic black, but the beautiful turquoise had caught her eye.

At exactly nine o'clock she stood at the front door and watched as Mick dug around in his duffel seeking his bathing suit. "I thought I left it in here, but I can't find it. Maybe I put it in one of the drawers with my underwear," he muttered as he abandoned the duffel bag and moved to the dresser.

Cassie fought the impulse to roll her eyes. First thing on the agenda and they were already going to be late. Typical Mick McCane.

"Aha," he exclaimed triumphantly as he pulled out black swim trunks with a red stripe down either side. As he approached where she waited he held them out toward her. "Mind putting it in your tote?"

She did so and then he opened the door and they were off. "I hope tonight is the night," she said as they stepped into the warm morning air. "I hope he comes after us tonight and we can wrap up this whole operation."

"It will happen when it happens." He slung his arm over her shoulder.

She stiffened at his close physical proximity and she knew he felt it. "I know, I know, relax," she said as she drew a deep breath and attempted to do just that.

He smiled at her, a genuine warm smile that shot a starburst of heat through her veins. "You're doing fine. Just act like you like me and don't hate me and everything will go smoothly."

"I don't hate you," she replied as they hit the sidewalk that would lead them to the spa.

"You want to talk about it now?" he asked.

"About what?"

"About what happened between us when we finished up the last case we worked together?" His arm around her shoulder seemed to tighten a bit.

She immediately tensed once again. "There's nothing to talk about. We slept together and then we got on with our lives."

He released a low rumble of dry laughter. "I have to tell you, I've never been kicked out of a woman's bed so unceremoniously. And you didn't just kick me out of your bed. You kicked me to the curb in front of your house and completely out of your life."

"I might have overreacted a bit," she admitted. "I just knew I didn't want a relationship and you'd made it clear you weren't looking for one and I felt like the whole thing had been a big mistake. Now, can we move on? Besides, the issue really had nothing to do with you, it was my problem."

"You want to talk about this problem?" he asked.

"No," she replied firmly. She didn't want to go into all the reasons sleeping with him had been a mistake. She wasn't willing to give up those pieces of herself to anyone.

Thankfully they were silent until they reached the spa, where they were greeted by a man named Tim Majors who introduced himself as the owner of the establishment.

Tim was a big man with a burly build and dark eyes. Although his smile appeared genuine as he told them about the natural hot springs that were reputed to have magical healing powers, Cassie noticed that the smile that curved his lips didn't quite ease a distracted darkness in his gaze.

"We have a public area where people can swim and relax, but most of our honeymooning couples prefer to choose a different experience in one of our eight private spa rooms."

"That's what we want, right, darling?" Mick said as he pulled her close against him.

She murmured her assent and Tim nodded. "Great, we'll set you up for an hour in the Safari Room." He turned and yelled over his shoulder. "Jimbo, we have guests." He turned back to look at them. "My son. He helps me out around here."

A big, lumbering teenager appeared at the desk. Like his father, he had dark eyes, but unlike his father no hint of a smile attempted to curve the sullen downward tug of his lips.

"Jimbo, please take our guests and show them to the dressing rooms and then escort them to the Safari Room. Make sure everything is ready for them there." Tim's voice held a definite tone of frustration and firm authority with his son.

Jimbo nodded. "Follow me," he said to Mick and Cassie. The big young man didn't speak again until they reached two doors, one marked Men's Dressing Room and the other with a sign that indicated it was the women's.

"When you're finished changing just wait here and I'll take you to the Safari Room," Jimbo said.

"So, you work here for your dad?" Mick asked.

Jimbo scowled. "Yeah. I thought I was heading out of this hillbilly town to college, but business has been so busy here my dad decided he needed me." He gestured toward the doors to the dressing rooms. "I'll be back in just a few minutes for you."

Cassie exchanged a glance with Mick as Jimbo lumbered back down the hallway. "Nice welcoming committee," she said as she tossed Mick his swim trunks.

"We'll talk later," Mick replied and then disappeared through the door.

The ladies' dressing room was huge, with a tiled shower area, two small saunas and a large steam room. Cassie entered one of the small changing cubicles and undressed. She tried not to think about the fact that within minutes she'd be half-naked with Mick.

At least the suit she'd bought was a one-piece, she thought as she pulled it out of her tote and stepped into it. Instantly she realized she should have tried it on at the store. What had looked modest on the rack looked anything but on her body.

The sides were high cut, exposing far too much of her thighs and derriere, and the neckline plunged downward to display an abundant amount of her breasts.

"Too late now," she muttered to herself as she neatly folded her clothes and put them into a locker. She slipped the locker key into the tote bag and then stepped outside of the dressing room door where Mick and Jimbo awaited.

Mick's eyes widened in obvious appreciation at the sight of her and she glared at him, daring him to make any kind of comment whatsoever. He simply grinned to show he'd gotten the message and then they followed Jimbo to their private spa room.

The Safari Room was exactly like it sounded, with wallpaper that looked like an African landscape, a large wooden sculpture of an elephant on a display stand and a lounging chair big enough for two in a leopard print.

The small pool in the center of the room bubbled and steamed and filled the air with the faint scent of sulfur and lavender. A tray with glasses of champagne and chocolate-covered strawberries sat on the edge, along with two large bath towels in the same print as the lounger chair.

"Enjoy," Jimbo said, although it was obvious his heart wasn't in it, and then he left the room and closed the door behind him.

"After you," Mick said and gestured to the pool.

"I think I'll just sit on the side and dangle my legs," she replied.

"I suppose you don't want me to mention how slamming hot you look in that bathing suit," he said as he eased himself down into the pool.

"I'd rather you not," she replied as she sat down and slipped her legs over the edge into the hot water.

"I suppose you'd rather talk about the fact that Jimbo isn't a happy camper working for his dad."

"I just wonder how unhappy he is," she replied. She wished he could get off the bench seat and sink all the way under the water instead of giving her a perfect view of his bare, muscled chest and his six-pack abs. "He's a big guy, it would be easy for him to shove his way through a door."

"You should really get in, this feels amazing." He closed his eyes for a moment and released a deep sigh. The only sound in the room was the bubbling of jets beneath the surface of the water.

This all seemed like such a waste of time. How could a killer see them inside this private little room? What was the point of the two of them being holed up here all alone? He didn't even act like he wanted to talk about the crimes.

"Relax, Cassie," Mick said without opening his eyes. "We've been in town less than twenty-four hours and I can feel the tension to get the job done coming off you in waves."

"I'm not used to sitting around and doing nothing," she replied.

He opened his eyes. "It might look like we're doing nothing, but we're doing exactly what we're supposed to be doing. Don't forget that it's possible at one of these places where it feels like we're just wasting our time, our killer could be sizing us up and making plans for the night."

"Jimbo goes to the top of my suspect list," she said, and finally decided to lower herself to sit on the bench just under the surface in the water. As long as it didn't go up over her head she was fine.

There was no question the hot water relaxed muscles she hadn't realized were tense. The strangely scented liquid felt like silk on her lower legs and thighs.

"It makes sense that somebody from the Black side committed the murders," he said.

"If you want to start screwing up the whole Honeymoon Haven madness, the best way to do it is to start offing honeymooning couples."

She wasn't sure if it was the right motive for the murders, but at least for now it was a working theory.

"I definitely want to check out that organization, and I'd like to somehow get a list of the people who belong to it."

"But I thought we were supposed to leave the investigating to Sheriff Lambert and his men. We're just the bait."

"But we aren't brainless bait and I don't intend to be completely blindsided by whoever decides to come into our room to kill us."

"So, we're investigating bait," Cassie said with an edge of excitement. This was what she did. Her job was what filled her life and gave her purpose.

For the next thirty minutes they talked about their plans to meet as many locals as possible, particularly those who were outwardly averse to changing the name of the town.

"It's a shame to waste these," he said as he gestured to the strawberries. He slid partially out of the water to sit next to her on the little bench inside the pool.

Acutely aware of his wet thigh against hers, the heat of him warming her more than the water, she fought the impulse to scoot away from him.

He picked up one of the strawberries by the stem and held it up to her lips. "Go on, take a bite," he said. "You never know who might be watching us at this very minute," he murmured, his lips separated from hers by the mere width of a chocolate-covered strawberry.

Cassie hated the fact that her heart suddenly raced and she wanted both to escape him and fall into him. She took a bite of the strawberry and as she swallowed the sweet morsel, his lips suddenly covered hers.

No, her brain cried, but her mouth wasn't listening to her brain. The kiss scorched through her with the fiery heat she remembered from kissing him before. It was only when he touched his tongue to hers in an effort to deepen the kiss that she pulled away, irritated with him and equally irritated with herself.

"I think you're taking advantage of this whole situation," she said. She stepped out of the pool, grabbed her towel and wrapped it around her, somewhat comforted by the cover.

"Maybe just a little," he agreed good-naturedly. He popped a strawberry into his mouth and then chased it with some of the champagne.

"I think I've had enough spa time," she said as he got out of the pool and grabbed the second towel.

"Our time in here is just about up anyway."

"I'm going to sit in the sauna for a short time, so I'll meet you in the lobby in twenty minutes," she said as they parted ways at the dressing rooms.

"Twenty minutes," he agreed.

Cassie's lips still burned from his hot kiss as she grabbed her locker key and dropped her tote bag on the wooden bench just outside one of the saunas. The bag held only her hairbrush, so she wasn't worried about anyone stealing it. Besides, at least for now, she was the only person in the dressing room.

She rarely got a chance to sit in a sauna, although she worked out as regularly as she could at a health club near her apartment. She entered the small wooden enclosure and sat on the bench inside.

No matter how hard she tried not to think about it, that darned kiss played and replayed in her mind. The fact that he'd admitted he was taking advantage of the situation only made it more outrageous. And yet he'd tasted so good.

Just like she'd remembered. Just like she'd

dreamed about for the past six months. No matter how hard she'd tried in the past couple of months, she hadn't been able to forget the way his lips had played on hers as he'd made love to her. Mick McCane might make her half-crazy, but the man definitely knew how to kiss.

She shifted positions and tried to shove all thoughts of Mick out of her mind at least for a few minutes. The heat inside the sauna felt intolerable, and her body quickly became bathed in a layer of perspiration. Breathing was difficult as the high humidity pressed tight against her chest. She'd never been in a sauna that contained this kind of intense heat.

She leaned her head back, thinking once again about the most recent kiss and the fact that Mick seemed reluctant to leave their past alone. It was probably all about his ego, she told herself. Mick wasn't the kind of man who would be kicked out of a woman's bed after lovemaking. Yes, it definitely had to be a male ego thing. He needed to make sure his charm and ability under the sheets hadn't been what had caused her unexpected reaction.

She gasped for a breath. This didn't feel right. Realizing the sauna was far too hot, too humid for her to handle, she got up and pushed on the door to exit.

It didn't open.

She pushed again, putting her shoulder into it and still the door didn't budge. What the heck? Was it somehow stuck? She pushed with all the force she had, but the door remained closed.

She fought against a sense of panic as the tiny room felt too hot to bear. "Hey! Hey, somebody help." She banged on the wooden door, but knew that there had been nobody else in the dressing room and she doubted her voice would carry outside of the dressing room area.

Her chest ached as she continued to draw in what had to be near-scalding air. She banged again on the door, yelling for somebody, anyone to come help her, but there was nobody, and after several moments of frantic banging she had to sit, her breaths coming in painful gasps.

Hadn't she read someplace about people dying in saunas? Her heart and lungs felt as if they were working triple-time just to keep her breathing.

The heat seemed not just to surround her but rather to consume her. She tried to get up once again to bang on the door but her body felt boneless and instead she leaned her head back and tried to keep breathing.

Chapter Five

Mick stood beneath a cool spray of water in the shower of the men's dressing room. He'd forgotten just how shapely Cassie was until he'd seen her in that bathing suit. She'd been stunning, and memories of how she'd felt naked in his arms, how she'd responded to his caresses, had dashed through his head. It had taken all his self-control not to respond to both the memories and the sight of her.

That kiss. He stuck his head under the water, allowing it to sluice over his face. He shouldn't have kissed her, but she'd looked so pretty and he'd wanted to so badly. It had definitely been a mistake, because he wanted to do it again...and again.

There was no question that she had major obsessivecompulsive issues, most recently displayed by her need to have the day's activities scheduled to the minute. It only made him want to dig deeper into her psyche and find out where she had come from, who or what had shaped her world.

In his household with his three older sisters there had rarely been a schedule, it had been living by the seat of the pants and rolling with the punches. That had certainly helped shape who he had become and how he dealt with the world around him. It was also what he believed helped to make him a good agent, the ability to change course, to go with the flow and make snap decisions without looking back.

He got out of the shower and dressed, knowing that if she said she'd meet him in the lobby in twenty minutes she'd be there. Not nineteen minutes, not twenty-one minutes, but precisely twenty.

He pulled on his dry clothes and then grabbed his swim trunks, wrung them out and left the dressing room. He not only liked looking at Cassie, but he also found her intelligent and stimulating. Her mind was quick and he liked that it challenged him to keep up with her.

And her lips had been pillowy soft against his and had tasted of strawberry and chocolate. He had to stop thinking about it, otherwise he'd need another cold shower before they left the building.

Tim greeted him as he stepped into the lobby. "Hope you two enjoyed your visit here," he said.

"We did, the waters are amazing."

Tim smiled easily. "And they are supposed to have medicinal healing properties."

"So, business is good?" Mick asked.

"Business has never been better. The best thing that ever happened to this town was Mayor John Jamison coming up with this whole honeymoon idea. You honeymooners sure saved my bacon. I was about to go bankrupt a couple of years ago."

"But I couldn't help but notice there's a movement against renaming the town," Mick said.

Tim's smile instantly turned into a scowl. "Derrick Black has divided the town with his nonsense of wanting to keep things the way they were. He's forgotten that half the businesses in this place were dying when we were just Black Creek…not even a dot on a map."

"So I'm guessing you're Team Honeymoon Haven."

"All the way," Tim replied.

Mick looked at his watch. According to the

time Cassie should be walking into the lobby at any second. Of course, they hadn't gone so far as to synchronize their watches. He smiled as he considered that it was probably just an oversight on her part.

He looked back at Tim. "It must be nice for you to have your son working here with you in the family business."

Tim snorted. "Jimbo would rather be out drinking with his buddies or chasing skirts than doing any real work. Kids today, they just want everything handed to them." He shook his head. "You and your bride, you planning on having kids?"

"Eventually," Mick replied, ignoring the sharp pang that pierced through his heart whenever he thought of having a child of his own. "But we're in no hurry."

"That's right, enjoy yourselves a long honeymoon phase before starting a family."

Mick checked his watch again. It had been well over twenty minutes since they'd parted at the dressing room doors. Where was Cassie? He knew it wasn't in her to take extra time to primp, especially knowing he was waiting for her.

"You'll spend half your life waiting on her," Tim said, obviously noticing Mick checking his watch. "That's part of our job as a husband…hurry up and wait."

Mick forced a laugh, but with each minute that ticked by a growing anxiety twisted in his stomach. "I think I'll just go knock on the door," he told Tim when thirty-five minutes had passed and she still hadn't appeared.

"Suit yourself. There are no other couples here at the moment. We usually get most of our business in the afternoons and evenings."

Mick heard the words as he hurried down the hallway toward the women's dressing room. Maybe he had Cassie pegged all wrong, he thought. Maybe she wasn't as much a stickler for time as he'd thought.

No, that wasn't right. He already knew her personality well enough that he knew with a gut certainty that she wouldn't keep him waiting this long. Something was wrong.

Something was definitely wrong.

His heart beat quickened as he reached the dressing room door. "Cassie?" he called, then banged on the door with his knuckles. He was vaguely aware of Tim appearing just behind him.

"Cassie, are you in there?" He waited another minute and there was still no reply. "Cassie, I'm coming in."

He pushed open the door and stepped inside, taking a moment to orient himself to the layout of the large area. The shower wasn't running and there was no sign of Cassie. He checked each dressing cubicle, a new sense of panic firing off as he saw her tote bag on a bench and her clothes neatly folded in one of the dressing rooms.

Her things were all here...but where was Cassie? A new panic seared through him. He raced to the shower to see if maybe she'd slipped and fallen and somehow knocked herself unconscious, but there was no body on the tiled floor.

A faint knock came from one of the saunas and Mick raced back toward it and tore open the door to see Cassie slumped against the wall, her entire body drenched and her eyes reddened and wide. The only sound was that of her labored breathing. "Mick," she finally managed to gasp.

In two short strides he was inside and lifted her into his arms. Hot. So hot. Not just the sauna she'd been sitting in, but her skin felt like it was in flames.

He carried her to the bench nearby. "Get me some water," he yelled at Tim, who immediately disappeared.

"I'm okay," Cassie said, her voice a weak whisper. "I just needed out... I needed to get out."

"Don't talk," he replied as she leaned heavily against him. She remained on his lap only a short time and then moved off to sit next to him on the bench. At least she was well enough to do that, he thought.

"I couldn't get out. I pushed and pushed on the door but it wouldn't open," she said. Her face was red, and even though he expected her to protest, Mick kept an arm firmly around her shoulder, as she looked too weak to sit upright without help.

By that time Tim had returned with a bottle of water. He handed it to Cassie, who unscrewed the top and tipped it to her lips. She drank greedily as Mick watched worriedly.

The sauna door had opened easily for him. Was it possible the intense heat had simply made her too weak to get out? "Are you all right?" Tim asked with obvious concern. "Can I get you something else?"

"No, thanks. I just want to get out of here," Cassie said after finishing the water. She got to her feet, slightly unsteady and Mick rose to grab her by the elbow.

"Are you sure you're okay? Maybe we should call a doctor," Mick said worriedly.

Cassie waved away the idea. "I'm fine." She forced a smile as if that alone would reassure him, but it didn't. "I just need to rinse off in the shower."

There was no way Mick intended to leave her alone again, at least not until he'd figured out exactly what had happened in here.

A moment later he waited just outside the tiled shower while Cassie stood beneath a stream of cool water. Meanwhile Tim checked the sauna door to see if there were any problems with it.

"I can't imagine what happened," he finally said to Mick. "I can't figure out why she couldn't just open the door."

"Is there another way into this dressing room?" Mick asked.

Tim frowned. "There's a back door, but we usually keep it locked." He left the sauna area and disappeared around the corner and when he returned his frown was even deeper. "The door was unlocked. Sometimes we get supplies through there and somebody forgets to lock up afterward. We had a laundry delivery this morning. I guess that's what happened."

By that time Cassie had finished in the

shower and had moved to one of the cubicles for dressing. It was obvious Tim was worried about repercussions, but Mick's sole concern was for Cassie.

"Needless to say, your spa time is on us today," Tim said as they all walked back toward the lobby.

"You definitely need to have somebody check the temperature in that sauna," Cassie replied, her face unusually pale. "Something wasn't right, it was too hot, too humid to bear."

"I'll check it myself," Tim said. "It's Jimbo's job to check the saunas and I'll have his hide if he screwed something up. And I'm so sorry that your experience here wasn't a pleasant one." He looked genuinely distraught. "I hope you both will give us an opportunity to gift you with another spa time."

"We'll have to see how our schedule goes," Mick replied. He grabbed Cassie's hand as they left the spa.

"There's no way we're going to work in another spa time while we're here," she exclaimed. "I've had all of the spa I want for a very long time to come. Where are we going?" she asked as he guided her in the opposite direction of the Stop the Madness headquarters.

"A change in plans," he replied. "Yesterday

I saw a little park and across the street from it was a deli. I'm thinking maybe a nice quiet picnic lunch in the park is just what we need."

She opened her mouth as if to protest a deviation from the schedule and then gave a slow nod of her head. "A quiet picnic lunch sounds perfect. It will give me time to process what just happened."

"We'll talk about it in the park. In the meantime the most pressing issue is whether you want ham and cheese or something else."

For the next few minutes they didn't speak as they walked down the sidewalk toward the little city park. True to Mick's words, a deli was just across the street.

Inside the deli they ordered sandwiches, chips and sodas and then made their way to one of the picnic tables under several leafy tall trees.

"Now tell me again exactly what happened in there," Mick asked as he unwrapped his sandwich.

"I got into the sauna and almost immediately realized it was too much for me. I pushed on the door but it wouldn't open." Her features showed the strain of that moment when she'd realized she couldn't get out.

"I pushed and pushed the door but it

wouldn't budge and then I started hitting the door and yelling for help, but nobody came." He noticed her hand trembled as she tore the cellophane from her sandwich.

What he wanted to do was pull her into his embrace, hold her tight until the trembling in her body stopped and the healthy color was back in her cheeks. But he didn't do that.

"Thank God you're one for punctuality. I knew when twenty minutes had passed that something was wrong." He gave her a wry grin. "You're never late."

"Thank God you came to find me. I felt like I was dying in there." She glanced up at the treetops, as if seeking some sort of answer that might be there. "It was like being inside a burning building." She looked back at him, her eyes holding the residual traces of fear.

"Is it possible you just got too weak to open the door?" he asked.

Her eyes were darker than usual as she watched him. "No way, there was something or someone keeping me from opening the door. I finally had to quit trying to push it open because I was getting weak, but not initially. When I first tried to push the door open I was fine. I was strong, but whoever or whatever was holding the door closed was stronger."

The very idea of this incident being anything other than an accident horrified him. "Maybe Jimbo decided to make a little trouble for his father," he suggested.

"Very possible. Nothing else makes much sense," she replied. "I will tell you this, the settings on that sauna were wrong. I've been in more than a few saunas, but nothing as hot as this one was."

For the next few minutes they sat and ate without talking. Several other couples joined them in the shady park, taking up tables nearby.

Mick's thoughts were jumbled with possibilities, none that he could twist around to make any sense. He couldn't believe this was the work of the killer that they sought.

It certainly hadn't been an effective way to kill anybody. It didn't fit the pattern of the previous murders. From Mick's experience, serial killers rarely changed their patterns.

No, this definitely felt more like a teenager's attempt to sabotage the family business. Jimbo hadn't exactly hidden his displeasure about working at the spa.

Still, he couldn't discount the fact that the

back door had been unlocked, allowing anyone to walk into the ladies' dressing room. That meant anyone off the street could have sneaked into the dressing room and tinkered with the settings on the sauna. That same somebody could have put their body weight against the sauna door, making it impossible for Cassie to push open.

According to what she'd said it hadn't taken too many attempts before she felt too weak and had given up. Is that when whoever had held the door had left the building via the back door?

One thing was certain, the original name of the town was the right one, for Mick sensed a darkness surrounding them unlike any he'd ever sensed before.

"SHALL WE TALK ABOUT the obvious?" Cassie asked as she grabbed another chip from the bag.

"What's the obvious?" Mick asked.

Cassie's heart banged hard against her ribs as she held his gaze. "The obvious would be that I haven't played my role right and that the killer has already figured out we're decoys and that the rules of the game have all changed."

All she could think about was how many times Mick had told her to relax, how often he'd had to remind her to look the part of a newlywed. He'd warned her that the killer could be watching them at any time. Had she already screwed up the assignment?

"I think it's a bit early to jump to that kind of conclusion," Mick replied, his tone surprisingly gentle.

"But it's possible," she said miserably. Failure. She felt as if she'd allowed her personal limitations to make this assignment a complete failure.

"And doubtful," he said firmly. He reached across the table and grabbed her hand in his. His thumb rubbed her skin in a soothing rhythm. "Don't beat yourself up, Cassie. All we know right now is that somebody screwed around with the sauna. Whoever it was had to have known that I'd get impatient and go looking for you. I don't think it was our guy. I doubt we've been here long enough or been visible enough to have even caught his attention yet." He gave her hand a squeeze and then released it.

"Thanks. I needed to hear that." She was surprised to feel the burn of tears at her eyes. She got up and threw her wrappers in a nearby trash can and then returned to the picnic table, her control regained. "I promise you from now on I'll do better."

Before he could reply, Sheriff Lambert and two of his deputies entered the small park, greeting people at the other tables and then approaching where Cassie and Mick sat.

"Afternoon, folks," Ed greeted them. "I see you two found a nice shady spot to enjoy lunch." He gestured to the two men on either side of him. "I thought I'd introduce you to two of my right-hand men." He laid a hand on the shoulder of the young, attractive deputy on his left. "This is Deputy Alex Perry," he said and then gestured to the man on his right. "And this is Deputy Ralph Gaines."

They all said their hellos and made a little small talk, and then the three men moved on to another table to chat with the tourists.

"Nice touch, having the local law friendly and accessible," Mick said. "How much you want to bet the mayor is behind the 'howdy folks' moments?"

"No bet, because I'm sure you're right," Cassie replied as the two of them got up from the table. "Unfortunately, if they're here schmoozing in the park, they aren't out actively working on the murder cases."

"True," Mick replied. "You want to head back to the room and rest a bit?" Mick's green eyes held a touch of concern.

"No way," she replied. "I'm fine, Mick, really. I think we should meander down the block and check out Derrick Black and his organization."

She was pleased when the concern in his eyes transformed to a hint of pride. She grabbed his arm and smiled up at him. "Come on, husband, let's take a little walk."

She was determined that she wouldn't be the cause of a failed operation. No matter how it affected her on a personal level, she would cuddle and snuggle up to Mick whenever they were out in public. She would be the perfect newlywed woman, hot and crazy for the man she'd married.

"Hmm, I could get used to this," Mick said softly as he wrapped an arm around her shoulder and pulled her tighter against his side.

"Public displays of affection only," she said lightly.

"Then I guess I'll just have to take advantage whenever we're in public," he replied with the charming smile that heated her from tip to toe.

She was determined that from here on she'd

play her role to a T and hoped that what she feared wasn't true, that she hadn't already screwed things up.

Within minutes they had reached the Stop the Madness headquarters. The door was open and they walked inside to see two dark-haired men and a young woman. The woman was on the telephone, one of the men was copying what appeared to be more flyers, and the other man greeted them and introduced himself as Derrick Black.

"This isn't really an establishment for tourists," he said. He was a tall, well-groomed man who had a deep voice that would naturally command attention. "This is about town business."

"We saw some of your flyers and were just curious," Mick replied.

A big man with arms the size of tree trunks appeared in the back doorway, his blond hair buzz-cut and his nose looking as if it had met more than one fist in its lifetime.

"It's all so confusing." Cassie released a light laugh and wondered if the big blond was a bodyguard. "I mean, I don't know whether to tell people we had our honeymoon in Honeymoon Haven or in Black Creek."

Derrick's eyes narrowed slightly. "Black

Creek, that's still the official name of the town and it will continue to be Black Creek if I have anything to do about it. My great-great-grand-father founded this town. Up until a couple of years ago it was a great place to live where people cared about each other and the crime rate was next to nothing."

It was obvious Derrick was on a roll, his eyes lit like those of a religious zealot, and his voice rose in volume with each word he said. The blond man stepped closer to where they stood.

"Since Mayor Jamison took office and came up with this brilliant idea of his, our crime rate has quadrupled, the business owners are at each other's throats vying for the almighty dollar and everyone has forgotten what a won-derful place this used to be to raise kids and live a peace life."

"How many people belong to your organi-zation?" Mick asked.

"We keep that information private." Der-rick swiped a hand down his jaw. "We're just working to make sure we regain some of the integrity of our town."

A deep frown tore across his forehead. "Look, this doesn't have anything to do with the two of you. This is a fight among the locals. Greed has turned people's heads and made them forget who they are, but that's our problem, not yours."

"From the looks of things you have a big battle ahead of you," Mick replied.

"It's a fight we're determined to win," the blond man said.

"Go and enjoy your stay here," Derrick said in an obvious dismissal.

"Well, good luck with your fight," Cassie said as she once again grabbed Mick's arm. "Come on, honey, you promised that you'd take me to that cute little dress shop."

"There's something just a little bit scary about him," she said once they were out on the sidewalk.

"He's definitely on my list of potential suspects in this whole mess," Mick agreed. "He and whoever is working for him."

"Did you see the size of that guy who appeared as soon as Derrick started talking to us? 'It's a fight we're determined to win,'" she said in a deep voice. "He was the second scary guy in the room."

"Yeah, I'd like to know if he's hired help or one of the local boys. He definitely didn't look like he does much paperwork. Why don't we head back to the room? I want to make a few calls and we can clean up and change clothes for dinner tonight."

"Sounds like a plan," she agreed.

"But first, we're going to head into a little dress shop and I'm going to buy you a pretty newlywed dress to wear to dinner tonight."

"That's not necessary," she protested and tried to decide if she should be offended that he didn't think anything she had in her suitcase was appropriate attire.

"But it is," he replied smoothly. "It's something both of our murdered couples did while they were here. Besides, it's something I want to do. It will remind me of home. My sisters are always dragging me shopping with them. They tell me I have a good eye for what looks great on a woman."

An hour later, as they headed back to the cottage with a new dress hanging in a bag, Cassie had to admit that his sisters were right. Mick had surprisingly good taste.

When they reached the cottage he sat on the love seat and pulled out his cell phone. He made a call to Rick Burgess. "Burgess, it's McCane. I wanted to see if you had done any investigation into the Stop the Madness organization and specifically Derrick Black."

As he listened to whatever the investigating agent had to tell him, Cassie went into the bathroom to get ready for dinner, certain that Mick would relay to her whatever he learned.

It was obvious the maid had been in. There were clean towels ready for use and she'd noticed a new fruit-and-muffin basket in the center of the coffee table.

As she took off her shorts and blouse, she realized it felt as if it had been months since she'd been in Director Forbes's office to learn her new assignment rather than just two days ago.

It was difficult to believe that in the last twenty-four hours alone she'd slept with Mick, shared a kiss, might have died and had a new dress that she never would have picked out for herself.

But she had no idea if they'd accomplished what they needed to. Had the killer homed in on them? Was it possible they'd already met him?

Was Jimbo angry enough at his father, at this town, to commit murder, or had the sauna episode simply been the work of a sullen teenager getting back at his father in a passive-aggressive fashion?

Was it possible Derrick Black would kill to keep the legacy of his great-great-grandfather? It was impossible to speculate on who the killer might be after less than two days of time in the town. To truly investigate they needed to talk to more of the locals, to get to know the players in the little drama that might be the motive for murder.

Shoving aside thoughts of killers, for the next few minutes she focused on getting into the royal-blue cotton sundress Mick had picked out for her. With its ruffled bodice, fitted waist and flared skirt, it was the most feminine piece of clothing Cassie had ever owned.

She touched up her makeup, brushed through her shoulder-length hair and stepped into a pair of gold-trimmed sandals she'd brought from home. Finally, she spritzed on some of her favorite perfume and then left the bathroom.

Mick whistled appreciatively at the sight of her. "I knew that dress was made just for you. You look…stunning…beautiful."

Beneath the warmth of his gaze, she felt like a woman who had specifically dressed to please her man and had accomplished just that. It was a strange, wonderful kind of feeling that she'd never experienced before.

"Give me five minutes and I'll be ready to

go." He grabbed a shirt and slacks from the closet and disappeared into the bathroom.

While she waited for him, she sat on the love seat and pulled out the folder that held all the crime-scene photos and reports, along with the notebook where she liked to keep notes.

She had to believe that the killings and the name change of the town were related. At least it gave a motive for the murders and it was one that made sense.

Somebody wanted to screw up the Honeymoon Haven image, and how better to do it than killing the loving couples who came to the town to enjoy their honeymoons? It was the only thing they'd stumbled on so far that held any merit as far as motive was concerned.

It was more like fifteen minutes before Mick came out of the bathroom, clad in a pair of khaki slacks and a white polo shirt. She looked up at him and tried not to notice how nicely the shirt tugged across his broad shoulders, how well the slacks fit the length of his legs. She patted the space next to her. "Come sit and tell me what you found out from Agent Burgess."

He sat down next to her and instantly she was aware of his smell, that heady combination of shaving cream and cologne. It elicited all those memories of the night they had shared, memories that were getting more and more difficult for her to keep out of her mind.

"Burgess told me Derrick Black and the people working at his organization are definitely on their radar. Black was interviewed by Sheriff Lambert but appeared to have alibis for the nights of each of the murders."

"What about Mr. Bodybuilder?"

"Jack Bailey, a homegrown thug. According to Burgess, Bailey is a nasty piece of work. He's had run-ins with the law since he was a young teenager and did a short stint in prison for battery. What are you doing there?" He gestured toward her notebook.

"Just writing some thoughts, impressions and facts in order to help me remember things I think are important about the case. I don't have the computer kind of mind that you do." She closed the notebook and leaned back. "You know I was just thinking before you came out of the bathroom that if the motive for this crime is to screw up the honeymoon madness, then he hasn't really been successful."

Mick frowned. "I'm not following you. He's managed to kill two couples and has gotten away with it so far. I'd call that a pretty good success."

"Yes, but there's been no publicity at all about the murders. Sheriff Lambert told us they'd managed to keep everything about the four murders under wraps for now. If you are trying to ruin a town's image, then wouldn't you want publicity that would make people think twice about staying here?"

"You're right," he agreed, in obvious surprise. "I hadn't thought about that. And what that means is we not only have a murderer who has taken out two couples, but we have a killer who must be extremely frustrated."

"Which would make him even more dangerous and perhaps ready to strike again at any moment," she replied. "And that's good for us." She released a small laugh. "I never thought I'd say that in my whole career."

He smiled. "I'm sure you never thought you'd be on a honeymoon with me in your whole career, either."

"That's definitely true."

They remained on the sofa for another half an hour, talking about motives and speculating on whether the murders had something to do with the name change of the town or something altogether different.

Cassie knew it was still possible that the man or men they sought might be thrill killers, with no real motive in mind except the enjoyment gained by taking somebody else's life.

It would be foolish for them to make any kind of an assessment about the killer given what little they knew. They both were too smart to settle on any one theory to the exclusion of any others.

It had grown dark by the time they left their cottage to head to the Wedded Bliss Buffet and Grill. "Looks like it's clouding up," Mick said as they walked down the sidewalk. "I hope that doesn't screw up the plans for tomorrow."

"And what are the plans for tomorrow?" she asked.

"A canoe ride down Black River, complete with a picnic for two on the banks of an outcropping named Kissing Point." He stopped walking and looked at her. "What's wrong?" he asked, obviously having felt the instant anxiety that struck her.

"I don't like water." She worried a hand through her hair. "In fact, I'm terrified of water." The anxiety grew bigger inside her although she tried to fight against it.

"All I can tell you is that I'll try to make

sure you don't even have to touch the water. I'm pretty good at canoeing. Can you swim?"

"Enough to take a bath, I'm not sure how I'd do in a river."

His eyes glittered in the deepening darkness of the night. "We'll make plans to go, but if you see the canoe and the river and decide you can't do it, then we won't." He took her hand and they started walking again.

"But it's something we need to do. The murdered couples both took the ride down the river," she protested. "That could possibly be the activity that brought them to the killer's attention."

"If we skip one of the activities on the list, the world won't come to an end," he replied easily.

They stopped walking again as they turned to cross the street where the Wedded Bliss Buffet and Grill was located. Cassie pulled her hand from his and gazed up at him. "We aren't skipping anything. We'll do the canoe thing and I'll be fine."

She swallowed against the nervousness that wanted to grab her by the throat. Tears of fear burned at her eyes as she thought of being in a little canoe on a big river.

Without waiting for Mick, she started across

the street, wanting just a moment alone to regain some control over her emotions. She
didn't want to be weak. She didn't want Mick
to perceive her as anything but a competent,
equal partner.

She was partway across the street when she
heard the squeal of tires against hot pavement.
The headlights of a car appeared out of nowhere and raced toward her, and she froze like
a deer mesmerized by the high beams.

Chapter Six

Mick saw the car and Cassie directly in its path. For a split second everything else around him fell away and he froze in disbelief.

Rather than brake, the car appeared to accelerate as it raced closer to where she stood in the center of the street. Adrenaline shooting through him, he raced to her and grabbed her by the arm. He yanked her back as the car whizzed by with the scent of hot oil and barely an inch to spare.

His heart pounded so loud in his ears that for a moment he could hear nothing but the frantic beat. He was vaguely aware of a crowd gathering around them and he held Cassie tight against him.

Her entire body trembled against his. As the sound of his heartbeat calmed, he became aware of her wildly racing heart. "Are you all right?" he finally managed to ask her.

She looked up at him, eyes wide and simmering with barely suppressed fear. She nodded. "I'm okay." She stepped out of his embrace. "Whew, that was definitely a close call."

"Probably some damn kid racing up the street," a man from nearby said.

"Did anyone notice what kind of car it was?" Mick asked, cursing himself for not noticing. He'd been so focused on Cassie he hadn't paid attention to anything else.

"It all happened so fast," a young woman exclaimed. "I didn't notice."

Apparently nobody had noticed anything about the car except that it had sped toward Cassie and would have hit her had Mick not jumped to action.

Mick pulled Cassie back into his arms as the crowd began to disperse. "Let's go back to the cottage."

"No way," she replied and once again stepped out of his embrace. "We're going across the street and eat a nice meal."

Her face was as pale as the moon and she wrapped her arms around herself as if to staunch the tremble that continued. "Are you sure you're up to it?" he asked.

"I can handle two near misses in one day, but I've got to tell you, Mick, this honeymoon is quickly turning into the makings of a reality show about honeymoons from hell." She offered him a small smile. "We stick to the schedule, and tonight we're having dinner at the Wedded Bliss Buffet and Grill."

"It's all about the schedule, right?" he said teasingly.

"That, and catching a killer." She grabbed hold of his arm. "And this time I'll let you escort me across the street."

Minutes later they were seated in the restaurant where both of them decided not to partake of the buffet but rather ordered off a menu. Once the waitress had departed with their orders, Cassie eyed him somberly.

"So, what do you think? Accident or on purpose? Was somebody trying to kill me or was I just in the wrong place at the wrong time?"

"My initial feeling is wrong place, wrong time, but we can't rule out anything," he replied. "I'd like to believe that it was probably just some dumb-ass teenager hot-rodding down the street without thought to pedestrian safety."

"That's what I want to believe," she said as she moved the salt and pepper shakers precisely to the center of the table. "The only thing that bothers me about the whole thing is that I never heard the squeal of brakes to indicate that the driver tried to stop."

"He or she didn't try to stop," Mick replied. His heart raced as he remembered that moment of seeing Cassie in those headlights, seconds from being splashed all over the street.

"Maybe whoever was driving was drunk or on drugs," she said.

"Possible. I intend to talk to Lambert to see if he's had trouble in the past with people roaring down the main drag. And now I suggest we take the next hour or two and just relax, enjoy our meal and talk about anything but speeding cars, hot saunas and murders."

He was rewarded by a smile that shot heat through him and flashed the memory of the taste of her lips into his brain. "Sounds absolutely perfect to me," she replied.

She leaned forward, unintentionally giving him a view of the creamy tops of her breasts. "So, tell me about these sisters of yours."

He picked up his wineglass and tried to ignore the wave of desire that burned deep in the pit of his stomach. He hadn't thought it would be so difficult to maintain his professionalism. But the pretend game of newlyweds was getting to him. *She* was getting to him and there was a battle being waged between FBI agent and man, and the man wanted Cassie in a way that had nothing to do with a working relationship.

"Mick?"

He focused back on the conversation, tamping down the hunger that had momentarily raged through him. "Lynnette is the oldest. She's forty-two and became a widow last year when her husband died in a car accident. Then there's Patsy, she's forty, married and has two children. Finally there's Eileen, she's thirty-eight, divorced and a single parent with one child."

"And they all doted on and spoiled you when you were little," she said.

Mick laughed. "They still do. I don't think they'll be satisfied until I'm married and have half a dozen kids of my own."

"But you've said you have no intention of ever marrying. Coming from such a family-oriented background, why wouldn't you?"

A small knot of tension formed in his check. "Let's just say I got close once and the whole experience left a very bad taste in my mouth. What about you? Was it a bad romantic experience in your past that turned you off the idea of marriage?"

She shook her head. "No, nothing like that."

She twirled the stem of her wineglass and then picked it up and took a drink. "I knew a long time ago that I wasn't the type to get married. I know my limitations, Mick," she said as she set her glass back on the table. "I know I'm obsessive-compulsive. I have a need to control my surroundings and I don't like the chaos and disorder that I know somebody else would bring into my life."

Mick studied her thoughtfully. "Must get pretty lonely in that perfectly controlled world of yours."

"Sometimes," she agreed. "But it's the world I choose, one I'm comfortable in."

The waitress appeared at their table with their orders, and for the next hour Mick regaled her with humorous stories from his childhood. He loved the sound of her laughter and sensed that she didn't allow much of it in her life.

What had happened to her that had made her design a world that allowed nobody in, that kept her cocooned by isolation? Was that why she had thrown such a fit when they'd made love, because he'd somehow threatened to invade the neat and tidy world she'd created for herself?

"Tell me about your childhood," he said

when they'd finished with their meal and lingered over dessert and coffee. "I've spent almost the whole time talking about mine, now it's time for you to share."

Her gaze as she looked at him was guarded, slightly wary. "I try not to think about it much. It was pretty awful."

"You were abused?" he asked softly. He wanted to somehow take away that guarded look in her eyes, the flash of torment that lit them.

"Not in the traditional sense of the word." She paused to take a sip of her coffee and then continued, "I mean, they didn't beat me or anything like that. My parents liked to party. Drugs, alcohol and rock and roll were their entire world." She gave him a bitter smile. "We lived like gypsies, always one step ahead of an angry landlord or a bill collector. I can't tell you how many times I was roused out of bed in the middle of the night to escape from paying rent."

"With only the clothes on your back," he said, realizing this was why she never unpacked, so that if she had to leave the room quickly she'd be able to grab her bag and have her belongings.

"Exactly." She picked up her fork and sliced

through the piece of chocolate cake she'd ordered, but before taking a bite she placed her fork back on the table. "I never knew what to expect from one minute to the next. I rarely went to the same school more than a few weeks at a time. Making friends was impossible. All I had was my parents...two adults who made bad decisions and lived like impulsive teenagers."

"Are they still alive?" Mick asked. He realized he'd just gained enormous insight into what forces had gone into the creation of the adult Cassie Miller.

"I don't know. The day I turned eighteen I left the motel where they were staying and I never looked back. I got my GED and once I turned twenty-one applied to the Kansas City Police Force. I worked myself up to detective and then applied to the FBI."

"And here you are," he said.

"That's right." She picked up her fork and took a bite of her cake, then chased it with a drink of coffee. "I've created my own world, a place where I feel safe, where I have all the control, and that's the way I like it."

Mick cut into his apple dumpling, remembering the night she had lost complete control. No wonder she'd hated him after that.

On that night he'd somehow managed to break through her shield, had battled through her defenses and what had come afterward had been a totally hot, totally spontaneous bout of lovemaking.

What made matters worse was that he wanted to breach her security again. He wanted to shatter her control and make love to her again.

This was all supposed to be pretend. He was playing a role with her, acting like her husband, her lover, and he knew it would be a big mistake to somehow blur the lines between reality and fantasy.

As they finished up their dessert he couldn't help but think about that moment when she'd been frozen in those headlights. Had it simply been an accident or had it been on purpose?

If it was on purpose, then who might want to target Cassie? The only answer was the unsub, and that would mean their cover was blown and the rules of the game had changed.

Worst of all, the only way he'd know for sure was if and when another attack occurred.

DAMN, DAMN. He thought he'd had her. She'd been standing right in front of him, frozen in his headlights, and in his mind's eyes he saw her splattered on the sidewalk, a dead honeymooner…a dead FBI agent with that shiny blond hair and those startled big, blue eyes.

It had been an opportunity that had been all gift-wrapped for him, one that he hadn't planned but rather had just presented itself. The moment she'd stepped from the curb alone he'd stomped on the gas, nothing in his mind except his need to hit her.

Her lucky rabbit's foot had been her coworker, who had managed to move quickly enough to pull her out of harm's way. He'd driven straight home and parked in his garage, cursing his failure, his second failure in the same day.

Screwing around with the sauna had been easy, and holding the door closed so she couldn't get out had been a piece of cake. He'd hoped to fry her nice and crispy, but in truth he'd realized the odds of her dying before somebody came looking for her was minimal. Still, it had fed his soul to hear her cries for help, to hear the utter helplessness in her voice.

He finally got out of his car and headed inside the house. Tomorrow was another day, and he was certain the right opportunity would present itself.

Still, his patience was growing thin. Each and every time he saw her she was an affront to his senses. Everybody loved a beautiful blonde with a bright smile and warm blue eyes, especially a woman they believed was on her honeymoon with her loving husband.

This was *his* town and he decided who lived and died. And newlywed Cassie Crawford, aka Special Agent Cassie Miller, was marked for death.

MICK AWAKENED LONG BEFORE DAWN, his heart pounding with the memory of the terror he'd felt when he'd seen Cassie in the headlights of that car.

If he hadn't pulled her to safety would the car have swerved to miss her? Had it been a teenage version of the game of chicken? He remained in the bed, smelling the sweet scent of her, listening to the sound of her soft, even breaths.

She was stronger than she appeared, much stronger than he'd initially given her credit for. And as crazy as it sounded he found her prim pajamas sexy as hell. The cotton top had little buttons that just begged to be unfastened, allowing her breasts to spill into his hands.

He slid out of the bed before he did something stupid and padded in the darkness toward the love seat. Once seated, he turned on the small lamp and opened the files from the original crime scenes.

He reread the reports, the transcripts of the interviews that had been conducted and then spread the crime-scene photos out on the table in front of him. He worried that somehow they were missing something. The idea that a local was responsible for the murders in order to screw up the newfound identity of the town felt too simple, too obvious.

Mick had always been suspicious of the obvious, and he couldn't halt the feeling that somehow they were all missing something important. Still, he reminded himself that sometimes it truly was the obvious, like the jealous husband killing the wife who'd left him.

It was just before dawn when he showered and dressed for the day, grateful that when he left the bathroom Cassie still slept soundly.

He scribbled a note on a sheet of paper from her notepad, left it next to her on the edge of her pillow and then walked out of the cabin.

Dawn was just beginning to streak across the morning sky as he headed toward a business he'd seen the day before. The air smelled fresh and clean and he enjoyed the solitude of the walk.

He had a feeling A Cup of Joe with Doughnuts opened early and he had a need to escape Cassie's presence for a little while, a need to gather his thoughts alone, without her nearness, without her very scent messing with his mind. The agents in the room next door would hear if anything went amiss in the room while he was gone.

The sidewalks were deserted, lit only by the streetlights at each corner. He walked leisurely in the fresh morning air and enjoyed the silence of a town mostly still asleep.

Just as he suspected, lights shone from the coffee shop and the front door opened to the scents of sugar and yeast and strong hot brew.

Straight ahead was a baker's glass display with a variety of doughnuts lined up to entice. There was a small countertop with stools and six wooden tables and chairs. As Mick approached the glass display a squat, older, dark-haired man appeared from a back room.

"Ah, an early bird," he said with an easy smile. "Tourist?"

Mick nodded. "Newlywed with a wife still in bed."

"I've got to warn you, I don't sell any of that

frappé crappy kind of stuff. You've got two choices for coffee, regular or decaf."

Mick grinned. "Regular, and why don't you give me one of those glazed. You must be team neutral," Mick said as he watched the man pour a tall cup of coffee in a disposable cup.

"Team neutral?" He looked at Mick curiously.

"You know, Black Creek or Honeymoon Haven."

He laughed, the sound deep and melodious as if he laughed often. "My name is Joe Cantelli. I've owned this business for twenty years and it's always been A Cup of Joe with Doughnuts and nothing's going to change that. I'll let all the other fools in town fight that particular battle. I've done just fine here without getting involved in all that crazy madness."

Mick paid for his coffee and doughnut and then slid onto one of the stools. "We've definitely heard the rumblings of the battle since we've arrived in town." He decided to take a chance. "I've even heard whispers that a couple was murdered not too long ago. Of course I didn't mention it to the wife. She'd freak out and I'd be in Hawaii or Niagara Falls."

Joe frowned and leaned with his elbows on

the top of the display counter. "I heard about the murders. The sheriff sometimes stops in here and a couple of his deputies come in here almost every morning, but I didn't know that the information was making the rounds out on the streets. Everyone is trying to keep it hush-hush. You know, bad for business."

"I suppose I listen to conversations I shouldn't," Mick replied easily. He took a sip of the hot, bold- flavored coffee. "So, you have any ideas who killed them?"

Joe's eyes narrowed slightly. "Are you some kind of cop?"

Mick laughed. "Me? Nah, but I'm definitely an armchair kind of detective. I watch all those crime shows and try to figure out who's guilty. I've already met a couple of people in town who look suspicious to me."

Joe gave Mick an indulgent grin and poured himself a cup of coffee. "Okay, I'll bite. Who do you think might be guilty?"

"Well, we had a little run-in with Jimbo at the spa yesterday. It was pretty obvious he hates all the honeymooning stuff as much as he hates having to work for his father."

Joe laughed. "Jimbo Majors isn't smart enough to work a fifty-piece jigsaw puzzle, let alone commit a couple of murders that has Sheriff Lambert stumped."

Mick bit into the doughnut and smiled in appreciation at the light sweetness in his mouth. He chased it with a drink of coffee and then continued the conversation along the same topic. "What about the folks over at the Stop the Madness organization?"

"That's not an organization," Joe scoffed. "That's Derrick Black and his brother Dan working with some hired help because they're desperate that folks will forget that they're very important people. Since he was old enough to wear a suit Derrick has paraded himself around town as the unofficial mayor, never letting people forget that we all wouldn't be here if it wasn't for his great-grandfather or whoever."

"Any other suspects on your radar?" Mick asked, hoping to get a name of somebody that might not have hit their own very short list.

"I just sell coffee and doughnuts, that's all."

At that moment the door opened and deputies Alex Perry and Ralph Gaines walked in. "Mick, right?" Alex said in greeting.

"That's right."

"You're an early one," Ralph said as he sat

at a table nearby. "Usually at this time of day Alex and I have the place to ourselves."

"I woke up and couldn't go back asleep. I didn't want to disturb the wife, so I took a stroll and found this place," Mick explained. He knew that both deputies knew he wasn't a newlywed but rather an FBI agent. They were playing the game admirably.

"This place is the best-kept secret in town," Alex said as he carried the two coffees Joe had poured to the table where Ralph sat. He eased down in the chair opposite Ralph and smiled at Mick. "You enjoying your stay here?"

"Sure, it's okay. My first choice was Hawaii but the wife saw some brochures about this place and you can see who won that battle." Mick shook his head ruefully. "Either of you married?"

"Not me," Deputy Perry said. "Got close a couple of years ago but it fell through."

"And I'm divorced," Deputy Gaines said. "I got to tell you there are some days seeing all the loving couples on the street makes me want to gag."

They all laughed and then Perry sobered. "There are days I think Sheriff Lambert feels the same way. He liked things better before Mayor Jamison got this brilliant idea."

"The sheriff would be okay if we could get more men on the force. He's just overworked and underpaid like we all are," Gaines added.

Mick looked at his watch. It was almost eight. Cassie would probably be up and he didn't think he could learn anything else here. "Gentlemen, it's been nice talking to you, but I need to get back to the motel." He finished his coffee and threw the container in the garbage can provided, then walked back to the display counter.

"Guess I'd better take a couple of these sweet treats to go for my sleeping beauty. What do you suggest?"

"The raspberry filled," Joe said without hesitation. "The ladies seem to love those."

Minutes later as Mick headed back to the Sweetheart Suites, a bag of doughnuts in hand, he wished the deputies hadn't appeared so early in his conversation with Joe. He had a feeling Joe could have added some names to their list of persons of interest if Mick had been alone with him for a little bit longer.

Maybe another early-morning visit to the doughnut shop was in order, unless, of course, the perp chose tonight to make his move on them.

He shoved away this thought, instead thinking about the schedule for the day. Thankfully the clouds from the night before were gone and the rising sun portended another hot July day. It was perfect weather for a leisurely canoe ride down the Black River.

As he opened the door to the room, he walked in to find Cassie in the bathroom. The bed was neatly made, his clothes from the night before were folded neatly on the chair and the note he'd written her was on the coffee table.

The room smelled of the coffee she'd made in the small pot and the faint whisper of her perfume. Her scent tightened the muscles in his belly in a not-unpleasant way.

He knew that today would be a difficult one for her. There was no way to control what happened on a river, and that would only add to her anxiety about being on the water.

He'd meant what he told her the day before. If they arrived at the landing and she found she couldn't do it, then they would turn around and come back here and figure out something else.

Mick knew about crazy fears. He'd rather face a knife-wielding maniac than run into an itty-bitty spider. Besides, being afraid of water when you couldn't swim wasn't a crazy fear at all.

The minute she stepped out of the bathroom she looked both beautiful and nervous, letting him know she hadn't forgotten the plans for the day.

"Good morning," he said. "I come bearing gifts." He sat on the love seat and patted the space next to him. "Grab a cup of coffee and see what I brought for you."

"You were rather cryptic with your note," she said as she poured her coffee. "'Gone, be back in a little while' doesn't say much."

She joined him on the love seat. She was dressed as casually as he'd ever seen her in a pair of denim jeans and a bright pink T-shirt that enhanced her blond coloring.

"I got up early and didn't want to bother you so I took a walk. I found a little coffee-and-doughnut shop and sat in there for a little while."

She opened the white bag and sighed with pleasure. "These look positively sinful."

"I was told by Joe, the owner of the shop, that raspberries were a girl's best friend."

She bit into the doughnut and rolled her eyes. "He was so right." She took another bite and a bit of the filling clung to the side of her lower lip.

He wanted to kiss it off. He wanted to lean forward and take her mouth in his, lick the sugary raspberry sweetness off her skin.

"So, you all ready for today?" he asked instead. "We're set up to take off from the canoe landing at ten. The weather is perfect for a lazy ride down the river. We'll be at the picnic area between eleven and eleven-thirty and after our lunch a car picks us up to take us back to the landing."

He was rambling and he couldn't seem to stop himself. He wanted to get his mind off his need to kiss her. "Of course, you know that if you don't feel up to the whole thing we can turn around and come back here and make other plans."

She popped the last of the doughnut into her mouth and wiped her mouth with a napkin from the bag. She then straightened her shoulders and eyed him with those amazing blue eyes that held both forced strength and a hint of vulnerability.

"I'm going to do this because it's part of our job. Besides," she offered him a smile, "I'm depending on you to keep me out of deep waters."

As he gazed into her eyes and then lowered his gaze to look at her tempting mouth, he wondered how in the hell he was supposed to keep her out of deep waters when, where she was concerned, he was flailing in deep waters himself?

Chapter Seven

The Honeymoon Haven Landing was a noble name for the tiny boat dock and rickety wooden bait shack that stood on the banks of the Black River.

As they got out of their car, Cassie eyed the river with trepidation. The brochure she'd read about it had indicated that the Black River had a slow flow with no rapids and few jutting rocks that made it perfect for leisurely canoe rides.

Still, as she eyed the murky water, all she knew was that the river looked deep and wide and potentially deadly. They were greeted by a tall, thin man in a pair of overalls who introduced himself as Jeb Manning. His skin was as brown as a walnut and his teeth gleamed white as he explained about their river adventure.

"About an hour or so downstream you'll come to a rocky inlet. You'll see some picnic tables there and that's where your lunch will be waiting for you. Have you all canoed before?"

"Never," Cassie burst out.

Mick smiled and laid an arm across her shoulder. "It's my bride's first time, but I've gone canoeing many times."

Jeb smiled at Cassie. "The secret is to just plant your butt in the center of the seat and don't move around much." He clapped Mick on the shoulder. "This guy looks like he's got it under control."

"I'm counting on it," Cassie replied fervently. As Jeb and Mick helped her step into the boat they'd be taking, her heart leaped to her throat with the rocking motion.

"Just sit," Mick said and pointed to the bench seat in the front of the small vessel.

She plopped her butt precisely in the middle of the seat and grabbed hold of either side of the canoe with her hands. Having successfully navigated getting into the vessel, some of her nervous tension eased, but it certainly didn't disappear altogether.

Mick stepped in and got seated without rocking the canoe, and with a wave to Jeb he began to paddle them out into the center of the river where the flow of the water would carry them along.

"Okay?" he asked. He looked at her worriedly.

She was almost afraid to nod her head, fearing that the simple motion might throw off their balance. "So far so good," she replied. "Shouldn't we have life vests?"

He pointed beneath her seat. "It looks like there's a couple shoved under there. Grab one for yourself. I don't need one. I'm a strong swimmer."

She pulled out one of the vests and wrinkled her nose in dismay. "Ick. It smells like fish and worm guts and has mold all over it." There was no way she wanted to pull it on.

He laughed. "You actually know what worm guts smell like?"

"Not really, but I think it smells just like this life vest. Maybe I'll just keep it here next to me in the seat where I can grab it if I need it."

He nodded and smiled. "Just try to relax and enjoy the ride."

She slowly released her death grip on the sides of the canoe and drew a deep steadying breath. "Okay, I'm going to try to relax."

"It should make you feel better to know that

this river ride was the last thing Bill Tanner and his wife did on the day of their murders."

"I know, and that means maybe our man will try to get to us tonight." She looked around. On either side of them was dense forest and lots of perfect places for somebody to hide, to watch and to plan. Still it was also impossible to ignore the stunning beauty of their surroundings.

"It's hard to believe that this kind of paradise could be hiding a killer," he said, as if able to read her thoughts.

As the canoe moved slow and steady, barely rippling the water, she truly found herself relaxing. "Even though we might be drawing the attention of a killer, this is kind of nice."

He flashed her that killer grin. "Sometimes trying new things, being spontaneous, and a little bit of chaos is good for the soul."

"I'm not sure you'll ever get me to agree to all that," she replied.

For a few minutes they floated, the sound of the water lapping gently against the side of the canoe and the call of birds overhead the only noise. Mick only paddled occasionally, allowing the natural pull of the river to take them downstream.

"Do you go canoeing a lot?" she asked, breaking the silence.

"I did a lot of it as a teenager, and in my early twenties, but then when I was about twenty-five I quit and haven't done a lot of it since then."

"Why did you quit?" she asked curiously. He appeared completely at ease in the canoe and handled the paddles adeptly. His features were relaxed in a way she hadn't seen before. It was obvious he loved being out on the water.

He frowned suddenly. "I quit because the woman I was engaged to at the time thought it was a foolish waste of time."

"The same woman who made you decide never to marry?" Cassie asked. She told herself she had no feelings for Mick, but she was suddenly ridiculously intrigued by the woman he'd once loved, the woman who had managed to break his heart. "Tell me about her."

He paused a moment and then released a deep sigh. "Sarah Batterson. She was beautiful and charming and the epitome of high maintenance." He paddled for a moment, a thoughtful frown still deepening a line across his forehead.

"Sarah and I were ill-fated from the beginning."

"Where did the two of you meet?" Cassie asked.

"At a charity function. Her mother was in charge of it and I was my sister Patsy's escort for the night. We met, started dating and the troubles began. Sarah didn't like what I did for a living, she came from a privileged background that I didn't understand. During the first six months or so that we dated, she broke up with me for some imagined slight at least a half a dozen times. She'd stay away for a couple of days, then come running back and I'd welcome her into my life again."

He shook his head. "It was like she mesmerized me. My sisters hated her. They told me she was manipulative and shallow, but I didn't want to hear it. I thought I was in love and I didn't want to listen to anyone who had anything negative to say."

"So, what happened?" she asked.

"She got pregnant and I proposed. I was going to ask her to marry me eventually, but the pregnancy just moved my time line up a bit. She started planning the wedding, everything seemed to be moving along smoothly and then we had another falling out."

For the first time since he'd started talking about her his features showed signs of stress.

A knot pulsed in his jaw and his shoulders grew more rigid.

"She accused me of not spending enough time with her. I was working too much and ignoring her. I knew she was being unreasonable but I figured I'd give her time to cool off and, sure enough, after a week she called me. She apologized for being a brat and told me she had a little confession to make. She'd been so angry with me she'd gotten an abortion, but she hurriedly assured me that we could still get married and have lots of babies later."

He stared at Cassie with hollow eyes. "Just like that she told me that she'd gotten rid of my baby, like she'd thrown out a purse or a pair of shoes that was out of season."

For a moment Cassie ached so deeply with his pain she couldn't find the words adequate to reply. She wanted to wrap her arms around his big shoulders, hold him close and somehow try to absorb the pain that darkened his eyes, the pain that had caused him to apparently forever close himself off to any future love.

He gave a dry laugh. "Needless to say it was at that moment that I realized I couldn't be in love with a woman that selfish. I broke off the engagement, moved on and never looked back."

"Not all women are like Sarah," Cassie said, finally finding her voice.

"I know." He paddled for a moment and then stopped. "But I've just never met a woman who completely takes my breath away, a woman who I know will love me as desperately as I could love her. I haven't met the one I want to share my heart with, share my life and soul with and until that happens, I'm a confirmed bachelor."

His sentence was punctuated by a loud ping. Cassie looked around to find the source of the strange noise. Had they hit something in the water? Maybe a rock? Did a canoe hitting a rock make that kind of a strange sound?

There was another high-pitched ping. A small hole exploded inward in the side of the canoe right in front of where she sat.

"Somebody's shooting at us," Mick said frantically as he jumped up. Cassie had a moment of sheer panic as she realized his sudden movement had capsized the canoe.

She plunged into the cold water, the life vest that had been on the bench next to her nowhere within her fingers' grasping reach.

She felt herself sinking, unable to see anything but murky water.

A new form of panic swelled up inside her, a panic born of her childhood experience of near drowning. Frantically, she flailed her arms and her legs in wild motions that did nothing to move her up or down, but rather kept her trapped in the watery depths.

She couldn't breathe. She couldn't find her way to the surface of the water. Up was down and down was up and water, water everywhere.

Hysterical laughter escaped her lips, appearing as a series of tiny bubbles that floated away, depleting part of the little bit of air she retained in her lungs. Somebody had shot at them. She was drowning.

Where was Mick? Had he been shot?

Was he somewhere floating in this watery grave with her? Was she all alone in the water? She could hear the sound of her parents' laughter and someplace in the back of her mind she knew she was dying.

A MILLION THINGS WENT through Mick's mind as he hit the water. The first was fear for Cassie. He knew she couldn't swim and he also knew that somebody from the opposite shoreline had shot at them.

He stayed underwater as long as possible, swimming in the area near the overturned canoe in an effort to find Cassie. With every second that passed his terror for her intensified. There hadn't been a chance to warn her that he was overturning the canoe. She'd had no opportunity to fill her lungs before she went overboard.

He broke the surface of the water, his gaze automatically going to the opposite shore to see if he could see the location of the shooter, to find out if there would be another shot fired.

He saw nothing but thick trees and overgrown brush, and no other shots were fired as his head remained above the waterline.

Cassie, his heart cried. He focused his attention on the water around him, seeking some indication of her whereabouts.

A frantic splash nearby sent him in that direction and he prayed it was Cassie and not an overactive fish. When he reached the spot he dove down, frantically searching…searching. He had to find her before it was too late.

He nearly cried in relief as he grabbed something and realized it was an arm…and the arm was connected to Cassie. He pulled her up to the surface, afraid that it had taken him too long, that she'd already swallowed too much water.

As her head rose above the surface, she released a gasp, spewed out a mouthful of water, and immediately grabbed him around the neck in a death grip that dragged them both back under the water.

He struggled against her desperation, aware that her frantic terror could be the death of them both. "Cassie, relax, I've got you," he exclaimed as they reached the surface again. "For God's sake, relax. I've got you."

Her wide panic-filled eyes darted in all directions, and then focused on him, and to his relief she went limp in his arms. "Lay back and let me take you to the shore," he said.

Obediently, she did as he asked, but once they hit the shoreline, he kept them both half in the water as he once again scanned the opposite shoreline.

"S-s-somebody sh-hot at us." Her lips trembled as if she were freezing, but he knew it was fear rather than any chill, as the sun beating down on them was hot.

"Stay low and head to those trees." He pointed to the nearby tree line.

"What about you?" she asked.

"I'll be right behind you," he promised.

As she got to her feet, he did the same, his body effectively shielding her from any other bullets that might fly in their direction.

When she reached the cover of the trees she collapsed on the ground, drawing in huge gulps of air as if she couldn't get enough. She wrapped her arms around herself and sat in a fugue of apparent numbness.

Mick kept his gaze narrowed to the opposite shore, seeking any movement that might indicate a person stalking them through the woods.

Who in the hell had shot at them? Had it been the killer? If so, then all the rules of the game had been changed. Their cover was possibly blown and they weren't safe anywhere anymore.

Dammit, they'd been so sure of how this all would go down he didn't even have a weapon on him. Both of their guns were locked in the car back at the dock.

He crept to where Cassie remained on the ground. Part of the color had returned to her face and she gave him a grim half smile. "If I don't get a chance later to tell you, thanks for saving my life." There was warmth in her eyes, a warmth that instantly threatened to pull him in.

"I just did what anyone would do under the circumstances," he replied gruffly.

"My parents didn't. When I was seven and they threw me into the deep end of a swimming pool, they laughed as I fought not to drown. Finally a man I didn't know who was staying at the same motel jumped in and pulled me to safety."

Rage welled up inside Mick, a rage coupled with a wealth of compassion for the child she had been. But he couldn't think about that now. He had to somehow get them across the river and to the dock before the gunman found them again.

There was no way of knowing if the shooter had a boat and had already crossed over to this side of the river and was now hunting them in the woods.

"We'll talk about how much I'd like to beat the hell out of your parents later, but for now we've got to move."

She nodded and pulled herself up to her feet. She drew a deep, steadying breath. "Ready when you are."

As they began to walk, Mick knew that Cassie was well aware of the danger. Her gaze kept shooting backward over her shoulder as if she expected somebody to come lumbering out of the brush with gun in hand.

The same sense of urgency thrummed through his veins. There was no mistaking those two bullets that had slammed into the canoe. Somebody had been specifically aiming at them. It definitely hadn't been an accident.

They paused only long enough for Mick to pull his cell phone from his pocket. He opened it and frowned. "Waterlogged," he muttered as he jammed it back in his shorts.

"Who were you going to call?"

"I was going to see if one of the other agents would pick us up someplace."

Cassie stifled a laugh with the back of her hand. "What were you going to tell him? Pick us up left of the big tree next to the other big trees?"

Mick grinned easily. "Okay, I admit it was a dumb idea."

They began to walk again. "How are we going to get back across the river and to the dock?" she asked worriedly.

"I haven't quite figured that one out yet," he admitted.

At that moment the silence was broken by

the sound of a motorboat. A new fear torched through Mick. Was the shooter now cruising the shoreline hoping to catch sight of them and finish the job he'd attempted?

His instincts told him to go deeper into the woods, but he ignored that survival instinct. He had to know who was in that boat. He needed some answers and taking the safe way might not give him any.

He motioned Cassie closer to his side. "Wait here, I'm going to check out who is in that boat."

Although she looked tiny and fragile with her wet clothes clinging to her and her hair just beginning to dry around her face, she raised her chin and nodded, an innate strength shining from her eyes. "Go, I'll be fine."

Mick moved with the stealth of a big cat toward the shoreline, his heart banging hard against his ribs. If it was the shooter in the boat he didn't want to give away their location, but he'd like to at least make some sort of identification.

The motor chugged at just above idle speed, indicating that whoever was driving the boat was going very slowly. This only increased the nervous tension that twisted in his gut as the water came into view.

The boat wasn't immediately visible to him and he had to creep out of the cover of the woods to look up the river in the direction from where they'd come to see it.

Jeb was behind the wheel and he was criss-crossing the lake, apparently looking for them. But Mick's gut instinct told him Jeb wasn't the shooter.

Mick stepped into the open and waved his hands in an effort to catch the man's attention. It seemed to take forever, but finally Jeb saw him and steered the boat toward the shore. Mick raced back to where Cassie waited.

"It's Jeb. I think he was looking for us. He's coming to pick us up."

Together he and Cassie walked back to the shoreline just as Jeb pulled up and shut off his engine. "Boy, are you two a sight for sore eyes," he said as Mick helped Cassie into the back of the small motorboat.

"How did you know we were in trouble?" Mick took the seat next to Jeb's.

"Your canoe washed up at Kissing Point, empty except for the two holes in the side. Jenna, my daughter-in-law, was there to deliver your lunch and when she saw the empty canoe she called me."

"Somebody took a couple of shots at us. We

had to dump the canoe and swim for cover along the shoreline," Mick explained.

Jeb looked at him in astonishment. "Jenna said there were a couple of holes in the side, but she didn't say they were bullet holes." His eyes narrowed as he scanned the opposite shore. "Probably a couple of drunken hunters. Dammit, it's not hunting season and that area is wildlife protected."

"Apparently those two little facts don't stop some people, especially if they've got a bit of liquid courage inside them," Mick replied, going with the hunter story rather than to admit to Jeb that they were chasing a killer who had apparently found them.

Jeb started his engine and within minutes they were back at the dock. "I'll reverse the charges on your credit card," Jeb said when they were all out of the boat and standing by the bait shop. "You didn't get the river experience you paid for."

"Don't worry about it," Mick replied, just eager to get into the car and out of there before somebody took a couple of shots at them again.

Mick didn't relax until they were back in the car and even then he didn't let down his guard.

They both pulled their guns from the glove box, ready for trouble if it found them again.

As they drove back toward the heart of town, he kept his gaze divided between the road ahead of him and the road behind them.

"Where are we going?" she asked as he passed the entrance to the Sweetheart Suites.

"I don't know about you, but I feel the need to get a little distance from Black Creek and gather my thoughts together." He looked over at her and couldn't help but notice that her nipples were hard against the damp T-shirt.

He tightened his hands on the steering wheel. He couldn't let his mind wander to the pleasures of Cassie. Adrenaline still pumped through him, making it dangerous for him to think about Cassie naked in his bed, his thumbs teasing those taut nipples. He had to keep focused on what had just happened, on what their next move should be.

"I figure we can find a place to stay in Cobb's Corners for the night," he said. "And then I want to set up a meeting with Sheriff Lambert for first thing in the morning. I need to update him on what's happened and I want him checking some alibis."

"What about clothes and night things?" she asked as she plucked at her damp T-shirt.

"I saw some kind of a discount store in Cobb's Corner close to the café where we ate lunch with Lambert. We'll stop there and they should have whatever we need for the night." Once again he tightened his hands on the steering wheel. He needed to get her out of that wet T-shirt as soon as possible.

They rode for a few more minutes in silence and he felt the weight of her gaze on him. "What?" he asked and glanced at her.

"It was *him,* wasn't it?"

Mick frowned thoughtfully before replying. "Yeah, I believe it was him."

"Then he's changed his pattern. He's completely changed the game." Her voice was taut with tension.

"Yeah, I know." A knot twisted in his gut.

"And you know what that means?" He didn't wait for her to answer, but rather cast her a quick somber glance. "We're now playing a game with no rules."

Chapter Eight

Cassie wasn't a happy camper. The discount store they stopped at didn't have her usual shampoo, the hairbrush she bought wasn't like the one back at their suite and apparently nobody in Arkansas wore long pajamas in July. The only night clothing she could find was a spaghetti-strapped, short, flimsy shift that was light blue and patterned with white sleeping kittens.

She added two pairs of new underpants to her small shopping cart and two pairs of shorts and two T-shirts, one to change into as soon as they landed someplace and the other to wear the next day. She then went in search for Mick who had been in charge of picking up toothbrushes and paste, deodorant and anything else he thought they'd need for the night.

She found him in the candy aisle, dropping several bags of goodies in his cart. "I thought you were getting toothbrushes."

He gestured to the bottom of the cart where a package of large white T-shirts, a package of boxers and a pair of black shorts rested next to the required items. "I just figured we might get a little munchy later. You like licorice?"

"I like these better." She grabbed a bag of chocolate-covered raisins and threw them into his cart. "Shouldn't we get holed up someplace before somebody from Black Creek sees us here?"

"Yeah, I'm ready," he agreed.

Mick paid with cash and within minutes they were back in the car and headed toward the Cobb's Corner's Motel down the street. The motel was located next to a fast-food place. Mick pulled up in front of the office and went in to see about a room for the night.

As he left the car, Cassie released a shuddery sigh that she felt as if she'd been holding in for hours. *You're okay,* she told herself. *You survived not only a crazed gunman, but also the Black River.*

She wasn't sure when she'd been frightened more, when she'd realized the hole in the canoe was from a bullet or when Mick stood up and she realized she was about to be cast into the deep river water.

But you're okay, she thought again. Still,

she couldn't stop the jitters that had seized her insides from the moment that hole had appeared in the side of the canoe.

You're a trained FBI agent, she reminded herself. *You can handle anything. Just whatever you do, don't fall apart.*

As Mick stepped out of the office, she couldn't help but admire the easy stride that carried him back to the car, the totally relaxed cast of his shoulders and the charming smile he flashed that lifted those sinful lips of his. Didn't he have the jitters, too? Wasn't he afraid of what might happen next now that they had no idea of the killer's next move?

Funny, but the very sight of him calmed her, steadied the nerves that had been jumping inside her since the unexpected dunk in the river.

He slid into the driver's seat and handed her a key. "We're in unit twelve. It's around the back, so our car won't be seen from the street." He started the engine. "And don't expect the same kind of accommodations that we've had at the Sweetheart Suites. I have a feeling business is tough here in Cobb's Corners."

"That makes sense. Most people would drive right by to get to Honeymoon Haven.

You don't suppose our killer is from here? Maybe a disgruntled business owner who every day watches his very livelihood zoom by?"

"It's something to consider, but my gut instinct is that our boy is from Black Creek." He parked in front of their unit. "The first thing I want to do when we get inside is tell the boys in the cottage next to ours that they can get a good night's sleep tonight because we won't be there. My phone should be dried out by now. And the second thing I need to do is to set up a meet with Sheriff Lambert."

They got out of the car, each grabbing some of the bags from the discount store. "I've never stayed at a place where I carried in plastic bags instead of a suitcase," she said as he opened the door.

He turned and smiled at her. "You've never taken a swim in a river, either. Just think of how this assignment and I are opening up your world."

"There are less dramatic ways to open up my world," she said ruefully as she stepped into the room. It was just what she'd expected. Gold carpeting, small nightstands, a round table and two chairs shoved in the corner and a television bolted down to the top of a small dresser. What she hadn't expected was the king-size bed.

She turned to look at him. "They didn't have any double-doubles available?"

"I'm sure they did, but I didn't ask." He dropped the bags he'd carried in on the foot of the bed. "Cassie, we don't know for sure that our cover has been blown. We still need to play our roles as a honeymooning couple, and honeymooning couples don't stay in separate double beds."

She wanted to argue with him, but realized he was right. They couldn't know for sure that their covers had been blown. All they really knew was that they'd definitely gained the attention of the killer.

She sighed and put her bags on the bed next to his. "Guess there's nothing left to do but get settled in."

"I'm going to make those phone calls and when I'm finished I'll walk next door and get us some lunch. I'm sure a burger and fries will be just as good as whatever would have been in our picnic lunch that we missed."

As Cassie carried one of the bags into the tiny bathroom, Mick got on his cell phone. A small sizzle of anxiety heated the pit of her stomach, the familiar burn when things didn't go as planned, when she had to fly by the seat of her pants.

She unloaded the items they'd bought, and as she did she remembered the conversation they'd been having in the canoe before the first bullet had struck, the conversation about Sarah and the baby that would never exist.

The selfish act of that woman had devastated Mick. She'd heard it in his voice when he'd spoken of it, seen the torment that had darkened his green eyes. Sarah had destroyed him, and there was a part of Cassie that wanted to make things right for him, that wanted to make him believe that love and family was still possible.

But she knew better than to entertain that kind of fantasy. She wasn't the woman to make his world right. She was obsessive-compulsive, a control freak who quivered at the very thought of change.

Mick was all about change, about going with the flow, greeting each day as if it were a great adventure. He was chaos and disorder and didn't fit with the neat and tidy and controlled world she'd built for herself.

Unable to wait another minute to wash off the river water, she turned on the shower and quickly stripped off the clothes that now smelled slightly fishy and would be making their way into the nearest trash can.

The hot spray of the shower coupled with the small bar of clean-scented soap the motel provided did the trick. She washed and rinsed her hair twice and then finally stepped out of the tub and dried off. There was no hair dryer, so she simply brushed through her clean wet hair and then left the bathroom.

Mick sat on the edge of the bed and smiled at her. "We're all set to meet Lambert at the Dew Drop Café tomorrow morning at seven. And now I want what you just had...a nice hot shower to get the river stink off me."

He grabbed a pair of shorts and his package of T-shirts and then disappeared into the bathroom. As he showered Cassie wandered the room aimlessly, checking the drawers in the dresser and the ones in the end table, finding nothing, not even the usual Bible.

He wasn't in the bathroom long, and when he reappeared he was in one of the new T-shirts and a pair of black shorts. "Ah, that's much better," he said. "And now to the really important stuff...lunch. I don't know about you, but I'm starving. Will you be all right here alone while I go next door for some food?" he asked.

She grabbed her purse and pulled out her revolver. "We'll be just fine," she assured him.

His eyes glinted with a teasing light that caught her breath in her chest. "God, you look hot right now."

"Get out of here before I shoot you," she retorted.

With a laugh he left the room. Cassie locked the door behind him and then wandered back to the bathroom and stared at her reflection in the mirror.

Hot? Hardly. Her hair was a straight mess from having air-dried without using any product or spray. She didn't have on a drop of makeup, but her cheeks filled with heightened color as she thought of the kiss they'd shared at the spa.

Drat the man anyway, she thought as she twirled away from the mirror. He wasn't her problem. His past was tragic, but everyone had baggage from their youth. You just had to suck it up and move on.

She unpacked the other bags and laid her new shorts and light blue T-shirt on the dresser. As she pulled out the nightgown, her heart jumped in an uneven rhythm. She'd never slept in anything quite so revealing, and the idea of doing so right next to Mick made her mouth grow dry.

With nothing left to do, she sat on the edge of the bed and tried to empty her mind from any thoughts of the night to come. Tonight would be no different than the past two nights she'd slept beside Mick. They were partners, not lovers.

Instead she focused her thoughts on everything that had happened since they'd first arrived in Black Creek, every person they had met and who she thought might be the culprit.

It was disheartening to realize they didn't have any real suspects, they simply had a couple of people who believed they might have something to gain if the town remained Black Creek rather than officially becoming Honeymoon Haven.

A knock on the door moved her to the window, where she peered out the curtain to see Mick holding a white sack and a drink tray. She unlocked the door to let him in.

"I almost ate mine on the way back," he said as he carried everything to the small round table in the corner. "I smelled the food and almost lost it." He began to unload the food. "I didn't think to ask you what you wanted so I got you a grilled chicken sandwich, a salad and a diet drink. If that doesn't sound good I got myself two big cheeseburgers and fries. I'll be glad to share."

Cassie sat at the table across from him. "No, chicken and a salad are perfect."

For the next few minutes they ate in silence. It was funny, she somehow felt closer to Mick than she'd ever felt to Glen. Maybe it was because Mick had shared with her his heartache. Maybe it was because they were facing an unknown killer and had only each other to depend on at the moment.

It was when they'd finished eating that they began to discuss the day's events. "I'm not convinced that we've been made as bait." He leaned back in the chair and frowned thoughtfully. "However, I definitely think the man or men we're seeking have identified us as a desirable couple for death."

"I was thinking about our suspect list while you were gone. Unfortunately it didn't take much thought because we don't have much of a list."

"True." He frowned thoughtfully. "We haven't had enough time to meet enough people to form a decent list. Let's just hope the agents tasked with investigating are doing a better job than we are."

"I was also thinking about how the perp got into the victims' rooms so easily, and Jimbo came to mind," she said.

One of his eyebrows raised in curiosity. "Tell me your thoughts."

I can't stop thinking about that kiss. I can't stop remembering how it felt to be held in your arms as we made love. I think you're an amazing man who couldn't be more wrong for me.

Of course, she didn't say any of that, but those were the thoughts that flew rapid-fire through her head. "I was thinking how easy it would be for Jimbo to show up late in the evening pretending that one of the couples had left a watch or some other personal belonging at the spa when they visited. Nobody would see him as a threat and they would probably immediately allow him into the room."

Mick nodded thoughtfully. "It's possible, but at this point almost anything is possible. I'm still betting that Derrick Black and his thug cohort Jack Bailey are looking good for this."

"How would any of them know we would be on the river today?" she asked.

"My best guess is that somehow we were followed." He blew a breath of obvious frustration and raked a hand through his thick hair. "There's nothing worse than being on a case where everyone else knows more than we do." He leaned forward, his annoyance obvious in the stern line of his jaw, the thinning of his lips. "I definitely want more information from Lambert tomorrow. I need to know all the players in this game, who he suspected initially and his gut instincts for these murders. He knows the people in town. I want his thoughts off the record."

"Sounds like a plan to me," Cassie agreed as she got up from the table and cleared off their trash. "It's going to be a long afternoon." She looked at the old television. "Somehow I doubt that thing picks up more than a couple of channels."

"We can always play cards." Mick withdrew a deck from his pocket. "I picked these up at the discount store because I knew we'd have some time to kill."

Cassie sat back down at the table. "What are we going to play?"

"Strip poker?" he asked with the expression of an eager puppy.

"In your dreams," she responded to his ridiculous suggestion.

"How about rummy?" He began to shuffle the cards as she nodded. "Don't you ever think about that night we spent together?" he asked as he dealt.

"Never," she lied and picked up her cards. "I told you before, that night was a mistake."

"Why?" His gaze no longer held a teasing light, but rather an intensity that let her know he didn't want a flip answer. He wanted the truth. "Why was it a mistake? We were both consenting adults and we both wanted it."

She needed to protest his words, to somehow make him believe that she hadn't been in her right mind that night, that it had been the alcohol that had made her not responsible for her actions. But that wasn't the truth, and he deserved the truth.

"You're right. I wanted you that night." She lowered her gaze to her cards, unable to look at him while she confessed. The queen of hearts stared back at her. "But I don't fall into bed with a man easily, and the last thing I'd want to do is to somehow get emotionally involved with you in any way. Intimacy can lead to other feelings. There's an old saying about kisses opening up the gateways to the heart."

"And you didn't want me to get hurt."

His words shocked her into looking up at him. She expected his eyes to be filled with that teasing light that had become so familiar and so charming. But instead, he looked serious.

A small burst of laughter escaped her lips. "On the contrary, I didn't want to get hurt. I didn't want either of us to attempt something that would never work. We weren't meant to be a couple, Mick, not anywhere except in this little pretend game we're playing right now."

"You're right, of course," he agreed as they began the card game. "I'd drive you crazy within hours if this were a real relationship. You've probably noticed I'm a bit of a slob."

"And I know I'm obsessive about things. I don't have an easygoing bone in my body. We'd be terrible together as a real couple."

"True," he agreed, and this time his eyes did shine with a teasing light. "But my sisters would like you. They'd think you were just what I needed in my life, a little order and control."

"And a little sanity," she added dryly.

He laughed. "I'm not crazy. I'm just used to being alone and being spoiled by my sisters."

"What would happen if they stopped spoiling you?" she asked.

He grinned, that sexy curl of lips that created a wonderful ball of heat inside her. "Then

I guess I'd have to learn how to pick up after myself and get more organized."

"You should try it some time, it's really very good for the soul."

"So is letting go a bit," he countered. "There's a time and a place to maintain control, but there are also times when it's okay to let go."

The conversation fell aside as they focused on the card game. One thing Cassie quickly realized they had in common was a fierce sense of competition.

He won the first game, she won the second and he won the last, and by that time, despite the fact that they'd munched on candy throughout the card games, they were ready for dinner. Once again Mick left the room to go to the fast-food place next door.

The later in the day it got the more she dreaded the time that she'd have to get into that little nightgown and crawl into that bed next to him.

Their conversation about the night they'd shared six months before should have been cleansing, but instead it had stirred up all kinds of crazy emotions inside her.

She wanted him again. The knowledge blossomed inside her with a kind of wonder. How was that possible? They'd sat together at the table and agreed that they were all wrong for each other. All she could expect from Mick McCane was wild, hot sex. No future, no relationship, just pure physical pleasure. As crazy as it seemed, at the moment that didn't seem so bad. After all, she didn't *want* anything more from him.

A wave of irritation swept through her. It was his fault. She'd always known he'd make her crazy and that's exactly what was happening. She was losing her mind.

She went into the bathroom and rearranged the items they'd bought on the countertop, trying to ease the jittery energy that filled her. She put his shaving cream, razor, toothbrush and deodorant on one side of the sink and her hairbrush, deodorant, toothbrush and hair spray on the other side. The toothpaste she placed just behind the faucet handle in the center.

Maybe this was all a post-traumatic-stress kind of reaction to the day. "That's it," she muttered to herself. She could have been shot. She could have drowned. She'd nearly been run over by a car and crisped in a sauna. Was it any wonder she was fantasizing about being held in big strong arms?

The rest of the evening passed with an excruciating slowness. They ate dinner, then turned on the television and watched an old rerun of a crime drama, both of them guessing who the killer was before he was revealed.

"Too bad it's not that easy in real life," Mick said. He was stretched out on the bed with pillows propped up behind his head. Cassie sat at the table watching the show while she played solitaire.

"You want the bathroom first or do you want me to get ready for bed first?" he asked when it was nine o'clock.

"Go ahead," she replied. "I'll go after you." The less time she had to wear that little nightgown the better. Hopefully if she took long enough to change and brush her teeth he'd be asleep by the time she got into bed.

She breathed a sigh of relief as he disappeared into the bathroom and closed the door behind him. There had been a tension between them since they'd played cards. Or maybe the tension was simply inside her.

She was too aware of him, the room was too small for his vibrant energy, his very presence. She felt half-suffocated by his nearness.

All she wanted was a good night's sleep. Hopefully the early-morning meeting with

Sheriff Lambert would give them more information and clarify what their next move should be.

He came out of the bathroom clad only in a pair of boxers and the scent of minty soap. The tension twisted tight in Cassie's stomach as she hurriedly grabbed her nightgown and clean panties and headed into the small room.

She brushed her teeth for a full three minutes and then she stepped into her panties and pulled the nightgown over her head. She stared at her reflection, her cheeks unusually pink as she saw the spill of her breasts at the plunging V-neck top and the length of her legs beneath the short, thin material.

She brushed her hair a hundred strokes and washed her face. Finally with nothing else left to do she exited the bathroom. Mick was on his back and he appeared already to be asleep.

She hurried to the overhead light switch on the wall near the door, turned it off and then in the darkness of the room made her way back to her side of the bed.

As she eased beneath the covers, Mick said nothing and his breathing remained deep and even. She should be glad that he was asleep, she told herself.

All was as it should be. Still, she couldn't stop the wild, wistful want that filled her as she closed her eyes and strove for sleep.

Chapter Nine

Mick wasn't asleep.

How could he sleep with her lying so close to him, filling the air with the scent of clean woman and the vanilla shampoo she'd used? How could he sleep with a vision of her in that sexy nightie, which had done little to hide her curves as she scampered across the room to turn out the light?

She was definitely getting to him and it wasn't just physical want that stirred him. As he thought of the childhood she'd survived his heart filled with admiration for the core of strength she possessed.

He liked the way her cheeks grew pink when he teased her, the fact that when he crossed a line she didn't hesitate to call him out. Yes, she was definitely getting under his skin in a way that should feel uncomfortable and have him running for the hills. But the strange thing was he didn't feel like running.

Sleep remained elusive as his thoughts turned to the crimes and those frantic moments earlier in the day. When he'd realized somebody was shooting at them, fear had roared through him, but after he'd capsized the canoe and couldn't find Cassie in the water, it had been sheer terror that had ripped through his very soul.

Oddly enough, when he'd told her about Sarah he couldn't remember exactly why he'd loved the woman, couldn't summon any feelings of regret that they hadn't made it as a couple. He'd long ago forgiven her for her selfishness, for not being the woman he'd wanted her to be. But he would never forget the baby who had paid the ultimate price for Sarah's impulsive, selfish action.

He rolled over on his side to face Cassie. Even though it was dark in the room, he could imagine her features relaxed as her deep breathing let him know she was soundly sleeping.

Sarah had been high maintenance and he knew that Cassie was high maintenance in a different way. Cassie probably had a life plan written down somewhere. She'd need to know where and why before any move was ever made.

The difference was he'd never be able to understand Sarah, but he understood Cassie. The glimpses of her childhood that she'd given him had let him know that she'd been a helpless victim to two adults who should have kept her physically and emotionally safe and secure. She'd spent years without control and now hung tight to it in order to feel safe.

He thought of those moments immediately after he'd pulled her from the river to shore. Rather than reaching out to him for comfort, she'd wrapped her arms around herself as if she'd never expected anyone to be there for her.

Even though his mother had died when he'd been young, his sisters had seen to it that he was surrounded by love. Cassie hadn't had that, and his heart ached for her.

A whimper sounded from her direction. Mick froze, wondering what images might be tormenting her sleep. He closed his eyes, knowing that if he didn't get some rest he'd be tired for the early-morning meeting with Lambert.

Cassie whimpered again, this time louder. The whimper was followed with a sob. Was she crying? He sat up, undecided if he should awaken her or let whatever dream she was having play out.

It was when she cried out and released a sob again that he made his decision. He quickly slid out of the bed and across the room to turn on the dim overhead light. She was curled up on her side, her cheeks damp with tears, yet she was still sound asleep.

Whatever her dreams, he didn't want her there. Dreams that made you weep could never be good ones. He got back into bed and then lightly touched her shoulder. "Cassie, wake up," he said softly.

She stirred but remained asleep. He shook her shoulder harder and her eyes opened. Her beautiful blue eyes stared at him with dazed confusion.

"You were crying," he said.

She closed her eyes and when she opened them again they were filled with the awareness of her surroundings and embarrassment. "I'm sorry. I was having a dream."

She sat up, and from the fact that she allowed the sheet to fall to her waist, exposing her shoulders and with her breasts half spilling from the low-cut nightgown, he knew she was still trapped in her dream.

"Want to talk about it?" Mick sat up next

to her, fighting his desire to pull her into his arms as she swiped the tears from her cheeks.

"It's just a dream I have about the past, about my life." She shrugged, looking achingly vulnerable.

Mick could stand it no longer. He reached out and pulled her back down to the bed and into his embrace.

She stiffened against him, but then with a deep sigh she relaxed and snuggled into the safety of his arms. He stroked the silk of her hair and felt the beating of her heart against his.

"I'm sorry, Cassie, that you didn't get the childhood you deserved. I'm sorry that you drew as parents people who should've never had a child."

"It was hard," she admitted. "I never knew what might happen next. They'd pull me out of bed for pancakes at two in the morning, make me miss school because they wanted me to help clean up a party mess. No day was ever the same. But it's over, I survived and we really should get back to sleep. Morning will be here before we know it." Although she spoke the words she made no move to return to her side of the bed.

Mick knew he shouldn't go there. What he

wanted from her as a man wasn't necessarily what she needed from him at this moment. But he went there anyway. He bent his head and took her mouth with his.

To his surprise she immediately opened her lips to him as if to encourage a deeper kiss. That was all it took for him to relinquish the control he'd maintained since the moment that they had arrived in Black Creek.

He wanted her and he tasted her hunger for him. As his tongue danced with hers, he rolled her to her back and stroked a hand across her delicate collarbones.

It was a prelude to touching her more intimately and when she didn't protest he covered one of her breasts with his hand. A small gasp escaped her as her nipple rose up to his touch, but she didn't protest.

Rather, she moved her hands up and down his back, his skin warming with each of her caresses. He moved his lips from hers and instead blazed a trail across her cheek and down the slender column of her neck.

"I want you, Mick," she said, her voice husky. "I know we aren't right together but just for tonight I want to be wrong. I don't want to be in control."

"I'll be glad to take control," he replied, inflamed by her words.

And take control he did. He kissed her until she was breathless. He smoothed his hands across the material that covered her breasts, impatient to touch her bare skin, to cover her nipples with his mouth.

With each kiss, with every stroke of his hands against her, he felt her surrender and the wildness growing inside her.

It didn't take long before his boxers and her nightgown were gone, thrown to the floor in a frenzy of passion. Bare skin met bare skin and Mick trembled with the need to completely possess her. Still, he didn't want to take her until he had fully sated her.

He wanted to make sure she would never forget this night as he had never forgotten making love to her the first time. She'd gotten under his skin on that night and he'd never managed to cast her out.

As he touched her panties she gasped and lifted her hips to aid him in removing them. Her eyes glowed dark and wild as his fingers sought to bring her pleasure.

He sensed the rising wave inside her as she raised her hips to meet his touch. He increased his pace as the room filled with the sound of their frantic breaths. She was beautiful in her wild abandon and watching her, touching her, had him hard and ready.

With a sharp cry she stiffened, tremors shuddering through her as she reached her release.

Instantly Mick moved between her thighs and eased into her moist warmth. He closed his eyes and remained motionless, overwhelmed by the sensations that roared through him.

She broke his inertia, bucking her hips upward as her hands grasped his buttocks. Slow and steady he stroked into her. He leaned down and once again captured her lips with his, reveling in the taste of her, the feel of her.

Their movements became more frantic, his strokes faster as he felt his climax approaching. She cried out his name as her muscles tightened around him. That was his undoing.

Waves of pleasure washed over him and he shuddered with the intensity of his release. He rolled to the side of her, momentarily breathless.

"Wow," she said.

He laughed. "Wow is right, and please don't ruin the wow by telling me that this shouldn't have happened."

"Why would I do that?" she asked with a

teasing smile. "We're both consenting adults who know the score."

Mick rolled over on his side to face her. "Friends with benefits?"

"Exactly," she replied as she slid out of the bed. "I'll be right back." She bent down and scooped up her panties and nightgown on the way to the bathroom.

As she disappeared, Mick rolled over on his back and stared up at the ceiling. He should be thinking about the case. He should be thinking about what their next move should be, but instead his head was filled with Cassie.

Friends with benefits, he'd never really liked that term. Either it was a relationship or it wasn't. He'd been guilty of casual sex with female friends, but for some reason in this case it didn't feel right.

She was predictable, a creature of habit, and was certain that relationships were messy and filled with the kind of chaos that would be intolerable. He released a deep, long sigh as he also realized he was precariously close to being madly in love with her.

THERE WAS NO AWKWARD morning after, but Cassie had begun to realize that nothing was awkward with Mick unless she made it so.

As they drove the short distance to the Dew Drop Café for their meeting with Sheriff Lambert she couldn't help but replay the night before in her mind.

It had been wonderful. It had been magic. More than that, as she drifted asleep in his arms she'd felt completely safe and secure, a feeling that was rare for her. He scared her because she never felt as if she got enough of him.

A part of her found it far too easy to desire spending every night in his arms, seeing that teasing light in his eyes over her first cup of coffee each morning.

"I hope the Dew Drop Café breakfast is as good as their burgers," he said, pulling her from her thoughts as he parked in front of the small eating establishment. He cut the engine and turned in the seat to smile at her, his eyes twinkling with a teasing charm that had once set her teeth on edge and now cast warmth over her. "I seem to have worked up an appetite overnight."

"I would've thought you satisfied your appetite overnight," she teased back.

His grin widened. "You definitely have potential, Cassie Miller. When you let yourself go and have a little fun, you take my breath away." He frowned suddenly and got out of the car.

Cassie hurried after him wondering what in the heck that was all about.

Lambert was already there at a back table with a cup of coffee in front of him. Greetings were made as Cassie and Mick joined him.

As Mick began to tell the sheriff about the various events that had occurred to them in the past three days, Cassie's thoughts immediately returned to the reason they were here.

Mick told the man about Cassie being trapped in the sauna, about the near miss with the car and finally about the near-death experience on the river.

Before Lambert could reply the waitress arrived to take their orders. "You should've called me the minute you got off the river," Lambert said once the waitress had departed.

"What could you have done?" Mick asked. "We didn't see the shooter and your men would've wasted a lot of time searching a thickly wooded area that wouldn't have yielded any clues."

"You don't know that," Lambert protested.

"The man we're after, or rather the man who is after us now, is far too smart to leave behind any evidence that might identify him," Cassie said.

Mick leaned forward. "Tell me, Sheriff, you know the locals in your town. You must have a gut instinct about who committed the murders. Maybe somebody who didn't make it into the official reports?"

Lambert took a drink of his coffee. He appeared to have aged since the last time they'd seen him. Weary lines cut out from the corners of his eyes and his frown appeared permanently etched into his forehead.

"I've got no evidence to tie anyone to these crimes," he said. "But my gut instinct is that Derrick Black has something to do with them. This whole town-naming issue has driven him over the edge."

"But he had alibis for the times of the murders," Cassie said.

"True. When the Armonds were murdered he was supposedly working late at his headquarters. A couple of his workers confirmed the alibi."

"Would they lie for him?" Cassie asked.

Lambert hesitated a moment and then slowly nodded. "Probably. Like I said, Derrick is desperate to keep the name of the town the same. His whole identity is tied into his relatives being the founders of the town, that the town is named after them…and him."

"Derrick Black doesn't strike me as the type who would actually get his hands dirty. What about Jack Bailey?" Mick asked.

"Derrick and Jack provided alibis for each other for the Tanner murders, and Jack's girlfriend said he was with her on the night the Armonds were killed."

"Is there anyone else on your radar?" Cassie asked.

"Not really," Lambert admitted. "We're a town of good people. We didn't have these kinds of problems before all the honeymoon nonsense." The waitress arrived with their orders, once again halting their conversation.

"I do intend to check some alibis for yesterday at the time you were on the river," Lambert continued as he cut into the thick piece of French toast he'd ordered. "Do you think your cover has been blown?" he asked before taking a bite.

Cassie looked at Mick. She was so afraid that if their cover had been blown then she was responsible. She hadn't played her role appropriately on the first day they had arrived in Black Creek.

"At this point I don't think he's made us as

FBI agents but we've definitely got his attention," Mick replied.

"So how do we move forward from here?" Lambert asked. "What do you two plan to do?"

As they ate their breakfast they discussed what the plans would be for the next couple of days. It was Mick's belief that the killer was deteriorating and the result was his abandonment of his pattern. He was losing control and now wanted, needed, Cassie and Mick dead as quickly as possible.

They kicked around the idea that it was also possible he was pushing a public killing to bring attention to the other two murders, to make sure that everyone in the area knew that it was no longer safe to honeymoon in Black Creek.

They left the café with a plan in place. Cassie and Mick would return to the Sweetheart Suites and resume their roles as newlyweds. Only now whenever they left their room they would be shadowed by two FBI agents for protection.

"Sheriff Lambert is definitely in over his head," Mick said as they began the drive back to Black Creek.

"He looks like a man ready to fall over from exhaustion," she replied.

Mick frowned. "I just hope we haven't fallen into some sort of tunnel vision by focusing on Derrick and Jack and the whole motive being about trying to destroy the honeymoon business in town."

"But that's all we really have at the moment that makes any kind of sense," she reminded him. "And Sheriff Lambert certainly had no other potential suspects to offer up."

She settled back into her seat and looked at the car clock. They would be back in Black Creek by ten. The whole day stretched out before them. "So, what are our plans for the rest of the day?" she asked.

He smiled. "I've been waiting for you to ask me that. I seem to recall on our list of activities was miniature golf. Feel up to it?"

"Feel like I could beat your ass," she replied with a smile of her own.

"Ah, a challenge. I hope you golf better than you play rummy."

They bantered back and forth playfully until they hit Black Creek's city limits and then they both grew somber. The game had suddenly gotten very real to Cassie. They were intentionally putting themselves out in the open and depending on others to keep them protected.

"Home, sweet home," Mick said as he pulled in front of their little cottage.

"It was supposed to be the point of attack," Cassie said as she got out of the car. She felt as if she had a bright red target on her back and didn't really relax until they were inside the walls of the suite.

"You look scared," Mick said.

"Aren't you?" she countered. "Even with a couple of agents shadowing us a bullet could come from any direction." She didn't mind doing her job, but she preferred to do it as safely, as smartly, as possible.

The room telephone rang, surprising them both. Mick answered, grunted a couple of times and then hung up. "That was Agent Sam Hunter from next door. The listening ears in the next cottage have heard your concerns and in just a few minutes one of those agents will be providing us a couple of vests to wear under our clothes."

"Then thankfully all we'll have to worry about is a head shot, and your big head makes a much better target than mine," she replied.

He narrowed his eyes in mock sternness.

"Maybe I liked you better when you didn't have a sense of humor."

She laughed. "What makes you think I'm kidding?"

Any reply he might have made was halted by a knock on the door. The same tall, sandy-haired man who had stepped outside of the cabin next door on the first day of their arrival stepped into the room with a large dark plastic garbage bag.

He introduced himself to Cassie as Special Agent Bob Hastings and then pulled two bulletproof vests from the bag. "It will be me and Agent Jacob Tyler shadowing you." He looked at Cassie "I've worked with Mick before and his fat head definitely makes a better target than yours."

A nervous giggle escaped Cassie. She immediately swallowed it as she took her vest and went into the bathroom to put it on beneath her blouse.

It would be easy to forget that their every word was being monitored by a team next door. Thank God last night had happened in Cobb's Corners rather than here. The idea of those agents next door hearing her every moan, each gasp that she'd made while making love was horrifying.

As she put on the vest, she had a feeling of a train rushing toward her. She suspected that the perp would make a move on them within the next twenty-four hours. His failed attempt at the river would have enraged him and he would be desperate to finish the job.

The end of the assignment was imminent and she should be glad, especially if the bad guy was caught and her and Mick were still alive. Besides, it would be good for she and Mick to get back to their own lives.

But instead of relief, the only emotion she experienced as she stared at her reflection in the bathroom mirror was loss, and the weary acceptance that soon she would be back in her neat and tidy and lonely world.

Chapter Ten

The Honeymoon Haven miniature golf course was as hokey a course as Mick had ever seen. The first hole had a bride and groom kissing and the goal was to hit the ball between them, and the second was a tall wedding cake with a hole in the top.

It was difficult to focus on the game while wearing a bulletproof vest and with two FBI agents lurking nearby. Cassie, too, obviously didn't have her head in the game. Her eyes were in constant motion, looking first one way and then the other.

If they'd been in a true golf contest they both would've lost, and by the fifth hole they'd stopped any pretense of keeping score.

As if afraid that she'd screwed up before, whenever Cassie wasn't looking around or putting the ball, she was all over him. She kissed his cheek and rubbed up against him and lit a fire inside of him that threatened to burn all of his concentration away.

"You're going to pay for this later," he warned her as she wrapped her arms around his neck and kissed the underside of his jaw.

"Just doing my job," she replied.

"Just warning you." He wrapped an arm around her back, holding her close against him. "You're starting something I'm going to want to finish."

"Fat chance." She danced away from him, her blue eyes teasing in a way that shot straight to his heart. "Besides, have you forgotten we have alien ears in our room?"

"Have you forgotten we don't have any ears in the bathroom?" He grinned as her face blanched and knew she hadn't thought of that.

As they finished up the game, Mick's thoughts flew a million miles an hour, jumbled thoughts about the case, about their suspects and finally about Cassie.

Their pretend love game was becoming far too real for him. It was becoming easy to imagine them together when this was all over.

Just his luck, he thought ruefully. The first woman he had believed himself in love with had been too needy, and the second woman he was falling in love with professed to want, to need, nobody in her life.

"I can't wait to get out of this vest," Cassie said as they walked back to their suite. "It's itching like mad and it's so hot I feel like I'm melting."

"We'll cool off for about an hour or so in the room and then around five head out to dinner at the Loving Couples Café." He knew she'd want specific places and times for the remainder of the day.

"Sounds like a plan," she agreed.

Once inside the room Cassie disappeared into the bathroom to take a shower and Mick removed his vest, kicked off his shoes and stretched out on the bed.

He closed his eyes and thought about their short list of suspects. Neither Sheriff Lambert's team nor his fellow FBI agents had managed to come up with any additional suspects.

However, they were all working under the assumption that the murders had been committed as some sort of statement against the potential name change of the town.

What if that assumption was wrong? That knocked everyone off their suspect list and left them with absolutely nothing.

It was obvious the killer had homed in on

Cassie and him, and that meant the only hope of catching him was when he made another attempt on their lives. The very idea of a killer after Cassie scared him to death. He knew she was a trained agent and he respected her ability as such, but as a man he had a fierce need to protect her from any danger.

She came out of the bathroom, and that surge of need welled up inside him, the need to protect her at whatever cost.

"Feel better?" he asked, glad that his emotions didn't alter the tone of his voice.

"Much." She sat on the edge of the bed.

"I was just thinking that maybe when this was all over it would be nice if we had dinner together back in Kansas City," he said.

She jumped up from the bed as if he'd goosed her and stared at him. "Why would we want to do that?"

Because I love you, because I don't want my time with you to end. I want more nights with you in my bed, I want more days seeing you smile, hearing your laughter.

"I don't know," he finally replied. "It was just an idea." He studied her beautiful features intently. "Would it really be so bad for us to have a relationship outside of this pretend one?"

She frowned and motioned him toward the bathroom. It was at that moment Mick remembered that their conversations were being monitored by the team next door. He'd gotten so caught up in his own thoughts, his own desires, he'd forgotten they had an audience.

He got up from the bed and followed her into the bathroom. She closed the door and then turned to face him, a touch of anger darkening her eyes.

"What do you think you are doing?" she demanded.

He shrugged. "I thought I was kind of asking you out on a date."

"But why would you even do that? You know I don't date."

"No, you skip right to the good part," he replied dryly.

"Low blow," she exclaimed with a swift intake of breath.

"You're right," he admitted with a touch of shame. "It was a low blow. I just... I just like you, Cassie. I like you a lot and I thought it would be nice to see you after this assignment is over."

She stared at him for a long moment, a nerve pulsing at the base of her neck. "We will see each other," she countered. "At the field office."

"You know that's not what I meant." A slight edge of frustration crept into his voice. "Would it be so awful if we tried it out together? If we actually date and see where it goes?"

"It would go straight to hell." She crossed her arms over her chest, her body language letting him know she was completely shut down. "We've had this discussion. We both know it would never work."

She was right of course, they'd talked about how it would never work between them, but at the moment he couldn't remember specifically why.

"Let it be, Mick," she finally said.

He shoved his hands into his pockets and leaned back against the glass shower door "I just think it's a damn shame, that's all."

She tilted her head to one side, her eyes narrowed with wary curiosity. "What's a damn shame?"

"That the parenting you got as a child is going to haunt you for the rest of your life, that you are going to hold on to your structure and control until you're an old, lonely woman." He pulled his hands out of his pockets, pushed off the shower door and left the bathroom.

He returned to his previous position on the bed and stared up at the ceiling. What had he been thinking? He shouldn't be surprised by her reaction to his idea of them dating. He'd come at her out of nowhere. Hell, he hadn't even realized he was going to say what he had before all the words had fallen out of his mouth.

Stupid. The whole thing had been a stupid idea. He'd allowed their roles here to get too deep into his head. He'd allowed her laughter to enchant him, her natural warmth to heat him, the core of her heart to touch his.

He just needed to finish this assignment and get back to his own life. He frowned thoughtfully as he remembered what Cassie had said about him, that he was spoiled by his sisters.

It was true. His house was cleaned, his clothes were washed and his meals were provided by his sisters. He was like a teenager with three doting mothers rather than a man taking care of himself.

Maybe he should take a few pages from Cassie's book, get more organized, take care of himself and tell his sisters it was time for them to back off and let him grow up.

He'd accused Cassie of allowing her past to dictate what her future would become, but wasn't he guilty of the same thing? After Sarah he'd shut himself off from the idea of any meaningful relationship with another woman and he'd maintained a thick case around his heart since then.

Until now. Until Cassie.

He'd been well on his way to joining her on Lonely Street, but something about his time with her had made him realize he didn't want that to be his final address.

He wanted love in his life. He wanted a wife and eventually a family. He would always be sad about the baby Sarah had aborted, but that didn't mean he didn't want the opportunity to have children.

Cassie had been his awakening, and his heart ached with the fact that she was determined to keep herself alone, to remain in her safe, uncomplicated world all alone.

At precisely five o'clock Cassie came out of the bathroom. Her slacks were navy, her blouse was red, and her mood was quiet.

"Are we not going to talk to each other?" he asked as they left the suite and headed up the sidewalk toward the Loving Couples Café.

He was aware of Agent Bob Hastings walking just in front of them and knew that one of the other agents would be behind them, but he was just as aware of a new tension between him and Cassie.

"We can talk," she replied, her voice exceptionally calm and controlled. "We can talk about the town, we can talk about the weather. We can even talk about the case, but all other topics are off-limits."

"If you're expecting some sort of apology from me then you're going to be disappointed." There was no way he was going to apologize for asking her out or for what he believed were statements of truth.

She released a weary sigh. "I don't expect anything from you, Mick."

They walked a bit in silence. The streets were clogged with couples laughing and chatting as they headed to a restaurant or an activity they would probably remember for the rest of their lives. Honeymoon happiness was everywhere, and yet somewhere amid the smiles and laughter, a killer lurked, waiting to take his next victims.

"You were right about one thing," he said, breaking the uncomfortable silence that had sprang up between them.

"What's that?" Once again her lovely blue

eyes held a wariness he knew that he'd placed there.

"I am spoiled. I've come to the conclusion that I need my sisters to take a step back from my life."

"You don't have to change your life because of something I said," she protested.

"I'm not," he replied easily. "I'm making some changes for me. It's past time. They need to live their lives without worrying about me. It's time they all stop thinking about me as a motherless little boy and let me grow up."

"Trust me, you're a grown-up," she replied dryly.

By that time they'd reached the café. In terms of cafés, this one was definitely up-scale. Although there was the requisite long and shiny counter, they were led to a booth covered in rich black leather.

As usual, the moment they were seated opposite each other, Cassie aligned the salt and pepper shakers side by side. It was a habit he now found oddly charming.

Bob Hastings took a seat at the counter and Mick assumed the other agent remained outside. Mick expected no trouble inside the café. The killer they sought was too smart to make a move in a public place like this where there were so many potential witnesses and he could be trapped inside.

A waitress appeared at their table with menus. They placed their drink order with her and then she left with the promise to return shortly.

Despite the excellent steak Mick ate, in spite of the fact that they lingered over coffee and dessert, the air between them remained strained.

Mick attempted some small talk but it took two to make a conversation and Cassie apparently wasn't in the mood. She made eye contact with him only by accident and seemed entirely pulled into herself.

"You know you have to get over being mad at me," he finally said with frustration. "We still have a role to play here."

She looked at him for a long moment and then leaned forward and covered one of his hands with hers. The smile that curved her lips upward shot a familiar flicker of fire through his veins. It wasn't just a physical reaction, but triggered a heart response, as well.

"Don't worry, I can do my job just fine," she said and then pulled her hand from his. She leaned back in her chair, her gaze lingering on him. "Besides, I'm not mad. I've just been reminded that blurring the lines between our professional and our personal lives isn't smart. I'm here to get a job done, Mick, and that's all. From here on out we have to keep it professional."

"Duly noted." He tried to ignore the surprising edge of disappointment that attempted to take hold of him.

As they left the café and headed back to the suite they hadn't gone far when they met Deputy Alex Perry and Deputy Ralph Gaines, who were obviously patrolling the streets as darkness fell.

"Evening, gentlemen," Mick greeted them. "Out keeping the streets safe for the tourists?"

"That, among other things," Perry replied.

"We've also been assigned to keep an eye out for potential victims that fit the profile... pretty blonde women and dark-haired men," Ralph said as he pulled off his hat and swiped at his forehead. "Even though Sheriff Lambert feels our man is focused on the two of you, he's worried that if he can't get to you he'll choose another couple, and we don't want that to happen."

Mick nodded. "I've worried about the same thing. I'd like to leave your town behind with nobody else being murdered."

"We'd all like that," Alex Perry replied.

They small-talked for several minutes and then Mick and Cassie continued toward their suite. "I hope it's us," Cassie said as they reached their door and she waited for Mick to unlock it. "I hope he's so focused on us he isn't even looking around at other people."

Mick opened the door and ushered her inside. "That makes two of us," he agreed.

"I think I'm just going to go to bed," Cassie said as she headed for the bathroom.

"But it's not even eight-thirty," Mick protested.

"It's been a long, stressful day. I'm ready to get a good night's sleep." She disappeared into the bathroom.

Mick knew she was escaping him by going to bed so early, but he felt wired and knew that sleep would be a long time coming. He turned on the small lamp next to the love seat and sat down, then pulled the manila file folder that Sheriff Lambert had provided for him.

Since he'd first looked at the information inside he'd worried that somehow they were all missing something important, that the evidence held a key nobody had picked up on. He'd read through the reports a half a dozen times, but now picked them up to read once again.

He'd only gotten through half of the background information on the victims when Cassie left the bathroom, wearing the sexy, cute nightgown with the kittens. He tried not to pay attention to her as she walked over to the switch that would turn off the overhead light.

"Do you mind?" she asked.

"Not at all. Will this lamp bother you?"

"No, it's fine." She shut off the overhead lamp, plunging the room into darkness except for the small pool of illumination around the love seat and coffee table.

He couldn't help himself. He watched as she crossed the room and got into bed, cursing himself for the conversation before dinner.

It was obvious that by asking her out, by indicating that he'd like a relationship with her away from here, he'd crossed a line. By doing so he'd destroyed the easy, natural relationship that had been building between them.

He frowned and turned his focus back on the reports. There was nothing in the victims' backgrounds that jingled any bells of alarm. Other than their close physical resemblance there was nothing else to interconnect their lives.

He moved on to the crime scene and evidence reports as a headache attempted to blossom at the base of his skull. The scent of Cassie wafted in the air, her clean, slightly floral perfume attempting to play havoc with his concentration. Rubbing the back of his neck, he reminded himself that he couldn't think about Cassie anymore other than in her role as his partner.

Realizing that the impending headache had gone away, he moved on to the crime-scene photos. They were gruesome memorializations of the last gasps of breaths the honeymooners had taken on this earth.

The headache he thought he'd circumvented reappeared, stretching taut across his forehead as he continued to study the photos.

Both couples had been in suites much like the one he sat in now. The two men were on their knees, slumped forward against the wall, each with a single bullet hole to the back of their heads. Quick, efficient death, he thought.

Professional.

Unemotional.

The descriptive words snapped through his head in a rapid rhythm.

The women were tied up on the beds, duct tape over their mouths, the front of their night-gowns crimson from the knife wounds that pierced their hearts.

Killing with a knife was far more up close and personal than killing with a gun. A knife to the heart was far different than the bullet to the back of the head.

Why use two methods of killing? Why one for the men and another for the women? Why not just shoot them all?

Quick.

Efficient.

Mick's heartbeat quickened. He thought about the events of the past couple of days. Cassie, somehow locked in a sauna. Cassie, nearly the victim of a hit-and-run, and the two bullets that had pierced the side of the canoe had been up front, where Cassie had been seated.

He stared back at the crime-scene photos. Had the men been wrong place, wrong time kind of victims? Had they been killed simply so the murderer could obtain access to his real, intended victims?

It was all about the women. The minute the words resounded in his head, he knew the rightness of his assessment.

The object of the killer's desires had not been the couples, nor had it been the men, but rather the petite blondes the men had married.

It was all about the women, the thought thundered through his brain again as his gaze shot across the darkened room to the bed where Cassie slept soundly.

This was a game changer. If his theory was right, then the killer wasn't focused on him and Cassie as a couple. His focus, his single goal, was to kill Cassie.

There was no way in hell Mick intended to allow her to be dangled as bait a minute longer. The fish that was after her was too smart, the risk far too big.

Chapter Eleven

"Cassie, hurry and get up."

The deep male voice shot familiar urgency through her dream, along with a horrible sense of dread. No, she mentally cried out. She didn't want to have to leave here. She liked it here. She'd even made a friend. No, Daddy, please don't make us run again.

"Cassie, come on. Sheriff Lambert is going to be here in just a few minutes," the deep voice said.

Sheriff Lambert? Cassie's dream fell away as consciousness began to take hold. She opened her eyes and squinted against the overhead light. Mick hovered over her.

"What are you doing?" she asked with a touch of crankiness. "What time is it?" Why had he woke her up in the middle of the night?

"A little after midnight. You need to get up and get dressed. Lambert is coming to take you out of here. You're off the case."

"What?" She shot upward. "What are you talking about?"

He tossed her a blouse and a pair of shorts "I'll explain everything after you're dressed. Now go."

She wanted to protest, but his features were taut with tension and his green eyes were dark. He didn't appear to be in the mood for any kind of an argument. She grabbed the clothing, slid out of bed and hurried into the bathroom.

Something had happened while she slept, she thought as she dressed quickly. But what on earth could've happened at this time of night that would have Director Forbes pull her off the case? And why was Sheriff Lambert on his way over to take her someplace?

Her eyes narrowed as she ran her brush through her sleep-tousled hair. Or maybe this was something a little more personal. She'd let Mick know she wanted nothing to do with him after this case was over and suddenly she was off the case?

She slammed the hairbrush down on the counter with more force than necessary. If Mick McCane thought he was going to somehow punish her for personal reasons, then he had another think coming.

She stepped out of the bathroom to find him standing at the front window staring out into the darkness of the night.

"You want to tell me what's going on?" she demanded.

He turned from the window to face her and although his features were still rigid, a flicker of something soft lit his eyes and then was gone.

"*We* aren't the target, you are, and that changes everything." He glanced back out the window and then back at her again.

"What are you talking about?"

He began to pace the room, energy coming off him in waves. "Think about it, Cassie. The men were shot but the women were bound and stabbed." He raked a hand through his hair. "I don't know why any of us didn't see it before. The men were simply collateral damage. The women were the desired targets."

Cassie sat down on the edge of the bed, trying to absorb this new information. "But this is just a theory of yours," she finally said.

"It's the right theory." His voice was strong with conviction. "We've had three close encounters with the killer. All three of those close calls involved you, not me."

Cassie stared at him as her mind went back

over the past couple of days. "But this really changes nothing," she finally said in protest. "We were sent here as bait and I'm still the bait."

Mick shook his head. "Not anymore. Both Director Forbes and I agree we need to back off and stash you someplace safe while we work through this new point of view. Sheriff Lambert is going to take you to the motel in Cobb's Corners where you and I stayed last night. You'll stay there until you get further word from either me or Forbes on where we go from here."

There was no more time for conversation as a soft knock fell on their door. Mick opened it to admit Ed Lambert, who was out of uniform and appeared to have just crawled out of his bed.

"Pack up whatever you need to," Mick instructed her. "At this point we don't know if you'll be returning here or not."

As Cassie went back into the bathroom to gather up her toiletries, she felt the same kind of helplessness she'd felt as a child. The world was spinning out of control and she had nothing to hang on to.

"Just go with the flow, Cassie." It was Mick's

voice that whispered in her head and she quickly packed up her toiletries.

The knot inside her chest relaxed a bit. She'd be fine in Cobb's Corners for the rest of the night, and hopefully tomorrow everyone would understand that she was their best chance for catching this killer.

She left the bathroom with suitcase in hand. Mick and Ed were seated on the love seat and both jumped up as she entered the room.

"An agent will be watching your room at the motel in Cobb's Corners," Mick said.

"Do you really think that's necessary?" she asked.

Once again, a softness whispered in the depths of Mick's eyes. "I'd rather have a little wasted manpower at work than have anything happen to you."

"Have you forgotten I'm an FBI agent and can take care of myself?" She said the words more harshly than she intended. When he looked at her like that he made her feel vulnerable in a way that had nothing to do with the killer's target on her back.

"No, I haven't forgotten," he replied smoothly. "But two FBI agents are always better than one. Besides, you won't even see the other agent if he's doing his job right."

"So, are we all set?" Ed asked, looking like there was nothing he'd like more at the moment than to crawl back into his bed.

"All set," Cassie agreed.

Ed opened the door and stepped outside. Cassie was about to follow him but was halted when Mick grabbed her arm.

"I'm sorry, Cassie. I'm sorry if I made you feel uncomfortable." He raised a hand and stroked his fingers down the side of her face. "Be safe," he whispered, and then he released her and gave her a gentle shove out of the door.

Thankfully, Ed didn't attempt any conversation on the thirty-mile drive to Cobb's Corners. Cassie didn't feel much like talking anyway. She did notice Ed checked his rearview mirror often, obviously assuring himself that they weren't being followed.

She stared out the passenger window into the dark of night. She wasn't afraid of being alone in the motel room, she figured the odds of the killer being aware that she'd been moved out of town in the dead of night were slim to none.

What scared her just a little bit was having too much time to think, too much time to think about Mick, and that was the last thing she wanted to do. Her cheek still burned from the softness of his caress.

"I'm sorry you had to get out in the middle of the night," she finally said when they hit the city limits of Cobb's Corners.

"No problem. It's part of the job." He turned into the motel parking lot. "I'm just glad to get you out of harm's way for now. We have planned a big powwow in the morning with my team and all of your fellow agents to see what the next move should be."

"We know I've already captured the killer's attention. You should put me back out there," Cassie said.

Ed parked the car in front of the motel office and then turned and gave her a rueful smile. "I have a feeling your partner won't want that."

"It doesn't matter what he wants. We need to do whatever is necessary to catch this person." While she appreciated everyone's concern for her, this was her job, and the job was all she had in her life.

Ed shrugged. "At this point I imagine I won't be calling the shots. I'm sure somebody will contact you sometime tomorrow to let you know the plan." He got out of the car and headed into the office.

He was back quickly with the key to the same room where she and Mick had stayed the night before. She would have preferred a different room, one that held no memories of the night they'd shared in each other's arms.

"Thank you, Sheriff," Cassie said as she got out of his car. She pulled her bags from the backseat and then unlocked the motel room door and turned back to wave at Ed.

He pulled away as she stepped into the room and closed and locked the door behind her. The silence of the room should have calmed her, but it didn't. She dropped her suitcases on the floor and sat on the edge of the bed, the same bed where she and Mick had made love.

She didn't want to think about that, nor did she want to think about the conversation they'd shared in the bathroom earlier that day.

She got up off the bed, went into the bathroom and quickly lined up her toiletries on the bathroom counter then changed into her nightgown. The bedside clock read nearly two, and even though she got into the bed, she had a feeling it would take her a very long time to go back to sleep.

She squeezed her eyes tightly closed. He'd asked her out on a date. He wanted to see if they could actually maintain a real romantic relationship when this was all over.

Crazy, her brain exclaimed, and yet her heart was less certain. There had been a part of her that had wanted to fall into the softness of his eyes. There was a part of her that knew he was right about holding so tight to control and order would eventually make her a lonely old woman. She hated to admit to herself that she was already a lonely young woman.

She must have fallen asleep, for when she opened her eyes again sunshine streamed in through the window and the clock on the nightstand read just after nine. She couldn't remember a time she'd slept so late.

Her first impulse was to jump out of bed, to get something accomplished, and then she remembered there was nothing for her to do. She remained in the bed and her thoughts instantly went to Mick and what they'd shared in this very bed.

There was no question that they were sexually compatible. She felt complete and whole when she was in his arms, and that scared her.

She hadn't expected Mick to be the man he was…a loving brother, a great shopper, a fun companion and a good and decent man.

She decided a long time ago to live alone,

to be alone because it was the easiest way to completely control her world. There were no surprises, nothing to fear.

Rolling over she hugged the pillow next to her, surprised to realize that control wasn't all that it was cracked up to be.

MICK, ALL THE FBI AGENTS and Lambert's team were all crowded into a small conference room. The room was overly warm, the air tense as Mick explained to them his new take on the murders that had occurred.

"This means everything we thought we knew about the murders is probably wrong," Mick said.

"But from what you've told us has happened to you and Cassie since you two have been here, it's obvious the killer wants her," Agent Jacob Tyler said. He grabbed one of the doughnuts provided by Sheriff Lambert out of the box in the center of the long table.

"So, wouldn't the easiest way to catch this creep be to put Cassie back out there?" Deputy Ralph Gaines asked.

"That's not going to happen," Mick replied, his stomach churning at the very thought. "I have no intention of putting Agent Miller into the line of fire. This situation is too volatile."

"Then how are we supposed to solve these cases?" Deputy Alex Perry asked, his frustration evident in his tone of voice.

"We all need to go back to the beginning," Mick replied. "We begin the new investigation focusing solely on women. We talk to every blonde woman in town, find out if anyone has hassled them, start a list of men who have had bad experiences with blonde-haired women."

"Hell," Alex Perry exclaimed. "I think probably each and every one of us here could put our name on that list."

All the men laughed and when they quieted Mick continued, "The man we're looking for is probably between the ages of twenty-one and thirty-five. We don't know yet what triggered him to suddenly start killing, but my guess is that our perp suffered some sort of trauma or dramatic event in the last year or so."

"So, you don't think this has anything to do with the mayor's attempt to change the name of the town?" Lambert asked. The sheriff's middle-of-the-night sojourn to Cobb's Corners showed this morning in the exhaustion that tugged his features downward.

Mick hesitated a moment and then shook his head. "No, my gut instinct tells me this is much more personal than that. However, we all need to keep all theories of the crimes in play."

The meeting lasted until afternoon and finally broke up with everyone being assigned a specific task. As the rest of the agents and deputies dispersed, Mick caught up with Sheriff Lambert before he disappeared into his office.

"Sorry about having to get you up in the middle of the night," Mick said.

"Not a problem. To tell you the truth, I haven't been sleeping that well since the first murder occurred," Ed replied.

"I have a slightly uncomfortable question to ask you," Mick said.

Ed motioned him into his office and closed the door behind him. "What's up?"

"I noticed there is an adult shop in town."

"There is," Ed replied slowly.

"It came to me last night after you left with Cassie." Mick shoved his hands into his pockets and gave the sheriff a wry smile. "It might be a stupid idea, but I was thinking maybe there was a way to pull Cassie back into the Sweetheart Suites without actually having her there."

Ed frowned. "What in the heck are you talking about?"

"A life-size blowup doll with blond hair that can be put on the love seat in front of the window of our suite."

Lambert's brown eyes narrowed thoughtfully. "I suppose it could work."

"The killer has taken a couple of shots at her before. She'd be a perfect target in that window. But I can't waltz into that store and buy one. I can't be sure that the killer isn't following me to get to Cassie."

"Understood. I have a lady friend who can take care of the purchase and arrange for one of the store employees to deliver it to your door. Nobody should get suspicious of the newlywed couple ordering a few toys to enhance their honeymoon pleasure."

Mick nodded in relief. "Great, I'll prop her on the love seat this evening and then I'll sneak out the bathroom window and watch what happens."

"You want extra men on this?" Ed asked.

"No, the fewer people skulking around the area, the better the odds that our guy will make a move," Mick replied.

"I'll get your new wife to you within the hour," Ed said.

With the arrangements made, Mick left the building and stepped out into the hot, humid afternoon. Instantly his thoughts flew to Cassie. He hadn't called her before the meeting, knowing that it had been a late night for them all. But now he needed to hear her voice, to assure himself that she had fared okay alone in the Cobb's Corners Motel room.

He waited until he got back to their suite and then sank down on the bed and called her cell phone.

She answered on the first ring. "I was wondering when you were going to call and let me know what's going on," she said, stress evident in her tone of voice.

"First things first," he replied. "How are you doing?"

There was a long pause. "I'm okay, I guess, although bored out of my mind."

"I'm sure it took you a few minutes to set up your stuff in the bathroom. Toothpaste, toothbrush, deodorant, hairbrush, gel and spray and finally your bottle of perfume. Always in that exact order, right?

"Are you making fun of me?" she asked crossly.

He laughed. "On the contrary, I'm letting you know that I pay close attention. I'll also have you know that I folded my own clothes this morning and made up the bed. I don't like the sight of an unmade bed."

There was a pause and then she finally replied, "Is there a reason you're sharing this with me?"

"I guess I just wanted you to know that an old dog can learn new tricks." He stifled a sigh. What he wanted to tell her was that if they both learned to compromise just a little bit they could share a world.

But he'd already flung his heart out to her and she'd pretty well stomped on it. He wasn't going to make the same mistake again.

"I suppose you'd rather me tell you that there's a potential that you'll be shot in the back of the head tonight." He explained the plan he'd devised and the high points of the meeting.

"Just don't get too cozy with your new bride," she said teasingly. "People will talk."

He laughed. "I like my women a little less plastic." He pressed his phone closer to his ear, wishing she was here beside him right now. "If my plan works then there's a possibility this whole case will be wrapped up tonight and tomorrow night you will be sleeping in your own bed."

"And not a minute too soon," she replied.

"Mick, I just want you to know that I've enjoyed working with you."

He held his breath, hoping there would be more to follow. But there wasn't. "Back at you," he replied with a forced lightness.

"You'll keep me informed how things go tonight?" she asked.

"Of course."

Geez, how had he become such a lovesick fool in such a short period of time? After hanging up with her, he paced the room, thinking about her.

She'd come at him out of nowhere, with a tragic past and a strength of spirit that stole his breath away. The lyrics to an old song blossomed in his head. He'd rather live in her world than live without her in his. Unfortunately she was in total control of what she wanted in her life, and he wasn't what she wanted.

His thoughts were interrupted by a knock on the door. He opened it to see a young man wearing the Newlywed Night Shop for Adults T-shirt, a bad case of acne and a smirk. "Your order," he said as he held out a large plastic bag.

"Thanks." Mick took the bag, gave him a tip and slammed his door, half-embarrassed that the kid knew what was in the bag. He could only imagine what he was envisioning the doll having to do with a newlywed couple's night-life. This case was taking him to places he'd certainly never been before.

It took him nearly an hour to pump up his new, slightly obscene companion. She had wide blue eyes and the requisite blond hair and Mick knew he'd have to anchor her down to a sitting position for this to work.

Once Plastic Cassie was ready for action, he stashed her in the bathroom until it was time for her to go to work later that night. With the rest of the afternoon stretching out before him, he decided to head down the street to the cof-fee shop and shoot the breeze with Joe. Who knew what tidbits of information he might be able to pick up there.

Unfortunately Joe wasn't working and a teenage boy was behind the counter. Mick ordered a tall cup of coffee and a couple of doughnuts and then left the shop.

On the way back to the suite he stopped in the Chinese restaurant and ordered sweet-and-sour chicken to go. Dinner and dessert, he thought as he made his way back to the cottage, and hopefully before the night was over…a dead doll in the window.

Chapter Twelve

Cassie spent most of her weekends home alone if she wasn't working a case and yet she'd never felt as lonely as she did now. She'd spent most of the day watching television and trying to keep thoughts of Mick out of her mind. But he was like an echo in her brain that refused to quiet, a haunting refrain of a song that wouldn't be forgotten.

He wanted a relationship with her when this was all over. He'd made it quite clear that he wanted them to explore something more than this assignment, something far more personal.

The idea both excited her and scared her half to death and she couldn't seem to get it out of her head. Even though she knew Mick didn't adhere to schedules, that life with him would always be filled with surprises and unexpected delays, there was a tiny part inside her that thought she'd be willing to put up with that to be with him, a part of her that wanted more from him.

The sex had been amazing, but just as exciting was the way he could make her laugh, how safe she felt in his presence, the kind of safety and security she'd never in her life experienced before.

Was it just a mirage? A vision of her own desperate need to have somebody she could depend on, somebody who would never let her drown in a pool or force her to run in the middle of the night from the place she called home?

She didn't want just anyone, her heart knew she wanted Mick. But her past, her fear, was greater than her want and he was right, that was a damn shame.

She had walked next door to the fast-food place at about four, for the first time seeing Bob Hastings behind her. She had no idea where he'd parked his car, didn't know what hidey-hole he'd found to keep an eye on her, but she thought his presence was an unnecessary precaution.

She was confident that the perp didn't know she was here in Cobb's Corners, that he would believe she was still with Mick at the Sweetheart Suites in Black Creek.

She ate in silence, the familiar silence of her life, and missed Mick's teasing comments, the sparkle of his eyes as he sat across from her at the table. She was shocked to realize the silence, the peace and calm, no longer felt as comfortable as it once had.

As darkness began to fall outside a knot of anxiety began to tighten in her chest. Would the perp take the bait? He'd shot at her before in the brightness of daylight. Would he take a head shot of "her" seated in the window of the suite, lit perfectly by the lights in the room?

Hopefully if somebody did shoot at the dummy doll, Mick would be nearby to grab the man and get him under arrest. Mick was right, it could all go down tonight and she could be back in her own bed, in her own apartment by tomorrow night. The thought should bring with it an enormous sense of relief, but it also brought a tinge of regret.

What might have been had she not endured the childhood she'd been handed? What might have been if she wasn't so afraid to reach out for something new, for something different than the way she'd lived her life as an adult?

She checked her watch. Just after seven. There was still about an hour and a half before complete nightfall and the killer probably wouldn't make a move until the whole town was sleeping.

Even though it was early, she changed into her nightgown and got settled comfortably in bed. She tuned the television to an old sitcom rerun with the volume set low. It was going to be a long night.

She nearly jumped out of her skin as her cell beeped to let her know somebody had texted her. WHAT R U WEARNG? It was from Mick and she couldn't help the smile that curved her lips and warmed her heart. He could be positively incorrigible.

NOTHG, she texted back.

Her phone rang immediately. "What do you mean, nothing?" Mick asked, his voice warm and slightly wicked.

"You asked, I told you."

"You're telling me tall tales, Cassie Miller. If I know you, you've got that nightgown on and are in bed covered up to your neck."

She smiled into the phone, pleased that he had called. "Actually, you're absolutely right," she agreed. "And what are you doing right now?"

"Waiting. There's nothing worse than waiting for evil to show up." The charm slipped from his voice. "I just hope this works, because we've got nothing on this guy and no other plans that might catch him."

Cassie sat up and pulled her knees up to her chest. "He's got to be ready to explode, Mick. If what we believe is true, then he's made three attempts on my life and has failed. He's got to be out of his mind with crazy, obsessive need."

"That's what I'm counting on," Mick replied. "Let's just hope he falls for the dummy in the window."

"I want you to call me if anything happens, no matter what time it is," she said. "I'd like to know the time of my alter ego's demise."

"Let's just hope it *does* happen tonight. Otherwise we have to figure out a new plan for tomorrow."

"We'll cross that bridge when we get to it," she replied.

"You're right," he agreed. "Well, I should let you go. I just wanted to hear your voice before the night truly began."

"I'm glad you called, Mick. Be safe tonight. Don't try to be a hero if things get too dangerous."

"Don't worry, my ego and self-love are way too great for that," he replied lightly.

"I'm serious, Mick. No heroics." Her heartbeat quickened at the thought of anything bad happening to him. Just because she was afraid to invite him into her life long-term didn't mean she wanted anything to happen to him.

"Promise," he said.

There was a moment of awkward silence.

"Cassie," he finally said. "I hope someday you find a man who you'll allow to get in, a man who can bring you happiness, give you the family you never had. I want that for you, Cassie."

A small embarrassed laugh escaped her, a laugh that to her horror ended on an unexpected sob. "Keep me posted, Mick," she said, and then clicked off.

Tears spilled from her eyes and she swiped at them, not understanding why she was crying. She'd known that Mick McCane was trouble the very first time she'd laid eyes on him. She knew he'd wreak havoc in her life. She'd just never expected to fall in love with him.

BY TEN O'CLOCK MICK had everything in place. The doll was on the love seat, bathed in the light of the lamp nearby. The window curtains were open to give the shooter a perfect view.

He'd sat next to it…to her…for about thirty minutes, pretending to talk, and then finally at ten-thirty he'd gone into the bathroom and out the bathroom window. The night air was warm as he dropped to the ground in the middle of some kind of bush.

He'd already decided his best view of the cottage and the general area was near the swimming pool. He could hide in the shrubbery that surrounded the pool area and see anyone who might come close enough to fire a gun at the woman in the window.

As he got into position and looked at the doll, he was surprised to realize that from this distance it looked like a person...it looked like Cassie. The blond hair was just about the length of Cassie's and hung straight and shiny like hers.

But nobody had hair as silky as Cassie's. Nobody had hair that held that sweet scent that stirred him in his very soul. His feelings were conflicted about the night to come. He wanted success in the assignment, but also knew that it would mean the end of his time with Cassie.

She was right, they'd run into each other at the field office, exchange pleasantries whenever they met. Eventually in the future they might even be assigned to work together again, but all of it would be sheer torture for him. They would never go back to the easy relationship they'd shared over the past several days.

The saddest part of all was that he knew she was capable of climbing out of the box her past had placed her in. He'd seen her get into a canoe on a river despite her fear, had seen her roll with the punches when their schedule had been shot to hell.

The problem was he couldn't make her believe in herself. Whatever demons haunted her sleep at night, whatever devils chased after her, had to be slayed by her. He'd love to be her white knight, but he couldn't play that role in her life unless she let him in, and she obviously had no desire to do so.

He settled into position at the base of the shrubbery, his gun ready in his hand. It was going to be a long night. He could hear couples still walking the streets, their laughter ringing out as the night began to die down.

It could be hours before anything happened. He consciously willed his thoughts away from Cassie and to the crimes that had occurred here.

He felt confident about his assessment that the women had been the prime targets, the men merely obstacles to get through in order for the killer to achieve his goal.

What still haunted him was how the killer had managed to gain entry into the cottages where the couples had stayed. There had been no sign of forced entry in either case, no open or broken windows, nothing to indicate that the killer had done anything except walk right in.

According to Lambert, all of the staff had been checked out at both locations where the murders had occurred and nothing had rung an alarm. But had Lambert been focused on the Black brothers and their organization to the exclusion of anything else? Mick definitely believed there was a dark personal element to the murders, that something had unhinged a man with a visceral hatred of blonde women.

Hopefully everyone working the case was reinterviewing everyone who had any contact with the murdered victims. Mick had stressed to all the men that morning at the meeting that it was vital they start all over again, this time focusing on somebody with a hatred for happy, beautiful blondes.

The minutes ticked by with agonizing slowness. The streets began to quiet and the night deepened. Mick shifted positions several times as he watched both the area around him and the plastic woman in the window.

At midnight his adrenaline began to build. If a murder was going to take place, he was guessing it would be within the next couple of hours.

His thoughts went back to one of the questions that had yet to be answered. How had the perp gotten into the rooms? He thought of the young man who had shown up at his door earlier in the day from the adult store. It would have been easy for him to allow the man inside the room, turn his back on him to dig a tip out of his wallet.

There had been no information about any deliveries the two couples might have had. He made a mental note to check into it the next day.

As the minutes continued to tick by, his frustration grew. *Come on,* he mentally urged. *Come on, you shot at her while we were in a canoe in the middle of a river. I've made it so easy for you here.*

Maybe too easy? Suddenly the whole idea seemed stupid. If the perp watched the woman in the window for any length of time he'd probably notice that she never moved, could probably guess that she wasn't a real person.

What had sounded like a brilliant idea in the middle of last night, tonight felt like stupid prank that nobody with any brains would fall for.

Mick would give it until two or so and then he'd go back inside and get plastic Cassie out of the window and they'd have to figure out another way to catch the killer.

By one his body was stiff, the heat, despite the darkness of night, was unrelenting, but he couldn't shut off his brain. Over and over his thoughts twisted and turned all the ins and outs of this case, trying to find the answers that had remained elusive.

Two couples dead instead of beginning their lives together. Four happy people cut down in their prime for reasons unknown. Lambert and his deputies had been working the case since the first murder a little over a month ago and no new information had come to light since then that would lead them closer to the killer's identity.

The law enforcement of Black Creek didn't appear to be incompetent and yet precious little in the form of evidence had been discovered so far.

Mick felt as if the past month of their investigation had been wasted time. They'd all been so focused on the motive of somebody fighting against the name change of the town, focused on specific suspects to fit that motive. Mick couldn't blame them. He and Cassie had initially made the same mistake.

Besides a delivery man or a employee of the establishments where the couples had stayed, who else could just waltz into a room and not make a woman scream, not force a man to fight?

Mick could understand a killer who was focused on a specific type of person, in this case pretty blondes. Maybe his mother was a blonde who'd abused him, or he'd been rejected by a woman with the same physical characteristics.

Mick had worked plenty of cases where obsessions were involved, where a killer focused on a specific type, imagined himself an avenging angel against evil, or retribution for pain inflicted on him.

This case had the same flavor. It spoke of a man's obsession. But who? And why? And how in the hell had he managed to get into those rooms without the couples feeling any sense of alarm?

There was only one other type of person who could appear at a door and gain immediate entry. Somebody wearing a uniform of importance...somebody like a sheriff.

Mick's heart seemed to stop beating at the thought. Crazy thought, right? He tried to tell himself that he was grasping at straws.

A vision of Ed Lambert burst into his head. The tired lines that radiated out from his eyes, the wrinkles that were deeply etched into his forehead—there was no question the sheriff was exhausted.

He'd complained of lack of funds, inadequate resources and not enough help. How deep did his resentment go of the new tourist traffic in town? He'd mentioned more than once that his men were pulling double shifts, that the crime rate had shot through the ceiling with the influx of honeymooners.

How desperate was he to get somebody's attention? A couple of heinous crimes threatening to undo the mayor's vision of the town might certainly force the mayor to up the ante for more money for the sheriff's department.

Lambert knew the plan for tonight, and nothing had happened here. It was almost two, and if the killer was going to strike then surely he would have done so by now.

The streets had been quiet for several hours, the only thing moving were the gnats that buzzed around Mick's head. It wasn't going to happen here. The words thundered in Mick's head.

Was he right about Lambert? He'd been in control of the investigations into the murders. He'd driven the direction that the investigations had taken. He'd made his sole focus the men who worked at the Stop the Madness organization.

Lambert knew what Cassie and Mick would have on their agendas. He'd known they would be visiting the spa, taking a canoe ride on the Black River. It would have been easy for him to hold the door of the sauna closed, to take those shots at them while they'd been trapped in the canoe. He could have even been behind the wheel of the dark car that had nearly struck Cassie in the middle of the street.

Nobody had checked Lambert's alibis for everything that had happened. Lambert had been in charge of the chicken coop.

Mick felt as if his head was about to explode. Right or wrong? Was this new theory the right one or was it his own desperation trying to identify a potential perp?

Hell, for all he knew Lambert had once had a blonde wife who left him. They hadn't talked about their personal lives at all.

Mick's heart beat quickly, new adrenaline flooding his veins. What if he was right about Lambert? That meant he'd sent the wolf to take the chicken to a "safe" place. If what he believed was true, then there would be no murder in Black Creek tonight, but there was a possibility that one would happen in Cobb's Corners.

With a sense of urgency, Mick left his hiding place and pulled his phone from his pocket. He punched in Cassie's phone number and waited as it rang three times and then went to voice mail.

Something was wrong. She would have answered, eager to hear how the night's events had played out. He raced toward the car in the parking lot. Cassie was in trouble and he was thirty miles away.

He had to get to her before it was too late, before the killer of Black Creek decided to take his act on the road.

Chapter Thirteen

Cassie had been pacing the small confines of her motel room since midnight, waiting for word from Mick, eager to hear the news that they'd caught the killer.

Several times she'd thought about calling him for an update but had immediately rejected the idea. He was probably in hiding, intent on the job, and she knew that if he had anything to report he would call her.

If they didn't get him tonight then she knew Mick was right, it was going to take old-fashioned police work to find the answer. They would have to go back to pounding pavement, reinterviewing anyone who had shared any time, no matter how brief, with the female victims.

It was possible she would be pulled off the case and sent back to Kansas City to begin work on something else. She'd been assigned to this case strictly because she fit the killer's profile, but there was no guarantee she'd remain since the bait had worked so well that the killer had changed his behavior and there was no longer a pattern to anticipate.

The part of her that was an FBI agent hated being taken off a case that wasn't finished, that hadn't been closed out, but the part of her that was a woman knew getting out of Dodge was the right thing to do, not because of any danger that might come from the killer but rather the danger that Mick posed to her life.

There was no question that he'd be a major disruption into her quiet, orderly world. He would destroy everything she'd worked so hard to build after escaping the chaotic madness of her parents.

Had she built herself into a box? Had she been so desperate to find order and control that she'd surrounded herself with a cage that held her captive rather than gave her freedom and peace?

If she allowed Mick in, it wouldn't all be crazy and wild. There would be moments of peace, moments when he held her in his arms and chased away her nightmares, times when she'd feel as safe as possible because he was beside her.

The last time they had worked together

it had been an intense week chasing a man who'd been killing prostitutes. They'd worked long and hard and there had been no time to talk about personal things, no time to get to know each other in any deep, meaningful way. Their sexual attraction to each other had ignited on the first day they'd been on the case and had simmered until the case had closed and they'd fallen into bed together.

This time was different. She'd admired Mick the agent, but now she knew Mick the man and he was so much more than she'd expected him to be. He had a wonderful sense of humor and when he spoke about his sisters a genuine affection rang in his voice. And when he looked at her, he made her feel like the most beautiful, desirable woman in the world.

With a sigh of frustration she sank down on the edge of the bed and traced the outline of one of the sleeping kittens on her nightgown. A glance at the nightstand clock let her know it was one-thirty. She was exhausted and yet amped with the restless energy that came from needing information.

There was nothing more she wanted than to hear her cell phone ring and Mick's deep voice telling her it was done, it was over. The bad guy was in custody and she and the people in Black Creek were safe once again.

It was all about getting the job done, and she had to keep it all about that. She couldn't think about Mick McCane the man anymore. Thoughts of what could be only made her head ache.

A knock on the door shot her up from the bed. Who would be at her door at this time of the night? She grabbed her gun from her purse and approached the window right next to the door. Moving back the curtain, the man in uniform standing there was visible in the light from the parking area.

She cracked open the door and lowered her gun. "Is it done?" she asked.

He nodded. "I'm here to take you back to Honeymoon Haven and Mick. I don't have all the details yet. The FBI moved in when the perp shot the back of the head of the doll, but that's all I really know."

"I've got to get dressed. It will only take me a minute." She released her hold on the door and stuck her gun back into her purse. "Come on in and I'll go get ready."

As he stepped into the room she threw her purse on the bed and then scurried into the bathroom and closed the door behind her. Except for the toiletries that were lined up on the bathroom counter, her suitcase was ready to go. She grabbed a pair of neatly folded shorts, her bra and a T-shirt and began to dress.

"You've got to feel great that this is all finally over," she said through the closed bathroom door.

"You have no idea," the deep voice replied. "It will be nice to get back to breaking up bar fights and dealing with petty crimes."

Back to normal business. Cassie wasn't even sure she knew what that meant anymore. The life she hadn't wanted to leave to take this assignment suddenly felt staid and empty.

Nonsense, she told her reflection in the mirror as she quickly brushed through her hair. She'd settle back in just fine when she got back to Kansas City. Nothing had really changed except she now had two nights to remember with a sexy, passionate man who had momentarily taken her breath away.

"Just another minute," she yelled through the door as she added her toiletries to her suitcase.

"No hurry. Take your time."

Most people would think the difficult part of the assignment was done. The bad guy had been caught and was now in custody. But

Cassie knew the most difficult part still was ahead of her. She had to tell Mick goodbye.

For a moment she leaned against the counter, weak in the knees as she thought of what she might be letting go of, the forever kind of love with a man she loved.

Her heart ached with the knowledge that she might be making a mistake, and yet her head rebelled at the thought of inviting him one hundred percent into her life.

He was right about her. The kind of parenting she'd gotten as a child had forever warped her for any other relationships. She would suffer a core of loneliness inside her because she was too afraid to let anyone in.

With a deep, weary sigh, she grabbed her suitcase and smaller overnight bag and stepped out of the bathroom. Deputy Alex Perry greeted her with a friendly smile. "All set?" he asked.

"All set," she agreed.

"Good, because I'm ready for the games to begin." He held out a gun with a silencer, his eyes narrowed to mere slits. "Now, get on the bed."

Cassie stared at him in horror as she realized they'd gotten it wrong. They'd all gotten it wrong, and now a real and present danger stood before her.

DOUBTS ASSAILED MICK as he pushed his gas pedal to increase his speed. He was afraid to go too fast. The road was narrow and twisted and he knew that a deer or some other animal could dart in front of him in the blink of an eye.

Had he chosen right? Was rushing to Cobb's Corners the right thing to do or should he have sat on the doll a little longer to see if the killer made a move?

But his thoughts kept going back to the question of who could have entered the murdered couples' rooms without any fuss. Who might be welcomed in and would have the power to subdue two people.

The answer kept coming back to Sheriff Lambert. Who knew what pretense he might have used to get inside the rooms? Mick had no idea what the true motive of the murders might be. His gut still told him it was something personal, but Lambert might have just been bringing attention to the mayor that they needed more funding, more manpower.

Of course, if that was the case then Ed Lambert definitely had a screw missing and that simply made him more dangerous. As he drove, the urgency that screamed inside him was tempered with thoughts of Cassie and the time they had spent together.

He loved her. But he apparently didn't have the tools to make her take a chance on him... on them. At their very core they were two very different people with different ideas about the world and how to function in it. But was that so bad? She had what he lacked, and he had the potential to give her what he thought she needed...somebody who would love her, somebody who would always be there for her.

He gripped the steering wheel more tightly, wishing he could fly to Cobb's Corners, praying that he was wrong about everything.

But the fact that he suspected Ed Lambert, the fact that Lambert had been the one who had driven Cassie to her motel room scared him to death.

Before leaving Black Creek, Mick had done a fast drive down the main drag, hoping... praying to see Lambert in his patrol car, but the sheriff had been nowhere on the streets. In fact, Mick hadn't seen a patrol car at all.

He hoped he was wrong. He prayed he was wrong. It was always particularly ugly when a member of law enforcement crossed over to the other side. Nobody ever suspected their lawmen to be killers.

None of the people working the case from the sheriff's office had been questioned, had raised a flag or had even been considered for a single second as a potential suspect.

He wanted to be wrong. He wanted to get to that motel room and find Cassie napping on the bed, her cell phone in her hand as she waited for a call from him to tell her it was finished. Maybe she was sleeping so soundly she hadn't heard the call he'd made to her minutes before.

Maybe she'd been in the shower…in the bathroom and hadn't heard her phone. That's why it had gone straight to voice mail. He desperately wanted that to be the explanation, but knew if that was the case she'd already have called him back.

Too late.

He was so afraid that he was already too late, that he'd walk into that motel room and find her bound on the bed, a knife wound to her heart.

God, he couldn't think about that. He'd rather tell her goodbye looking into her eyes than say farewell by placing flowers on a grave. With this thought in mind he increased his speed once again.

The minutes ticked by in excruciating increments, the miles passing far too slowly despite the speed he tried to maintain. Twice he was passed by cars going the other direction. Neither of them were patrol cars from Black Creek.

Too late. His brain screamed the two words, forcing a headache of stress to stretch across his forehead. Too late. He'd waited too long to realize what might be happening. It had been hours ago that he'd last talked to her. It had been hours ago that he'd last seen Ed Lambert.

Fifteen minutes out from Cobb's Corners and it felt as if he couldn't get there fast enough, like the remaining distance was traveling to the moon.

Please make her be okay. He'd been wrong before and he desperately wanted to be wrong this time. It didn't matter that she couldn't love him the way he wanted her to. All that mattered was that she was alive and well and would go on to live a happy life under her own terms.

Any other alternative was simply unacceptable. Please, let her be okay. Please, let me be wrong, he prayed as he sped toward the small motel in the small town of Cobb's Corners.

"DEPUTY PERRY...ALEX, you don't want to do this," Cassie exclaimed as he taped her ankles together with duct tape. He'd already warned her that if she screamed he'd shoot her and there was a wild darkness in his eyes that made her believe him.

He could shoot her dead and nobody would hear the sound. She was vaguely surprised that everyone in the entire state of Arkansas couldn't hear the frantic beating of her heart.

Her hands had already been bound in front of her with the duct tape. "I can help you," she said softly. "We can get you help for killing those other people, but if you kill an FBI agent there will be no going back. They will come at you with everything they have."

He smiled at her as he finished wrapping her ankles. "They have to find me before they can do anything to me." He leaned close to her, his eyes glittering with a hint of pride. "I'm not on their radar. In a million years nobody is going to suspect me. And I've been smart, Agent Miller. I haven't made any mistakes."

"This is a mistake." Cassie fought to keep the sob that threatened to rise up the back of her throat from releasing. She had to stay calm and she somehow had to gain control of the situation.

There was no way to get to her gun, no way

to move from the bed unless she simply rolled to the floor. She had only her wits to work with, and hoped to try to break through to him, to get him to surrender.

He leaned back from her, his gaze turning contemplative. "You look just like her," he said softly.

"Like who? Who do I look like, Deputy Perry?" She used his title on purpose, hoping to reach the man inside him who had taken a vow to uphold the law.

Besides, every minute she could keep him talking was a minute he wasn't stabbing her to death, was time she could use to try to figure out a way out of this disaster. Her phone had rung half a dozen times and she could only hope that it was Mick and he would grow concerned when she didn't answer. But he was thirty miles away and at least for now she was in this all alone.

"Tiffany," Alex said in answer to her question, stress thick in his voice.

"And who was Tiffany?" Cassie asked softly. If nothing else she would die with the answers they'd all been seeking…why had four people been killed?

"Tiffany Maxwell. She was my fiancée." He hovered over Cassie, the gun still held in his hand. "We were supposed to get married. It was all set, the plans all made, and we were going to honeymoon right here in Honeymoon Haven. It was our special little joke, that we didn't have to leave home to get the total honeymoon experience."

His voice rose and his handsome features tightened into a mask of rage. "We were supposed to be one of the happy couples walking the streets, laughing with each other and staying in one of the fancy suites." A sob caught in his throat but his eyes once again narrowed. "And before all that could happen she changed her mind about me...about us. She destroyed my dreams. She killed me."

"But you have to know that murdering those women, killing me, doesn't punish Tiffany, it doesn't change anything," Cassie said.

Once again he leaned down, his face close enough to hers that she could spit at him, and she fought the desire to do so, to somehow vent her disgust, her terror, in any fashion.

"Oh, but it does change things." His breath was hot on her face. "It makes me feel better. And now I'm tired of talking."

As she realized what he was about to do, she opened her mouth to scream, but before the scream could release from her he slapped a piece of duct tape across her mouth and smiled. "And it appears you're done talking."

He straightened and shoved his gun in his waistband and then withdrew a wicked-looking knife. The sharp edge gleamed in the lamp from the nightstand and the sight of it caused a frantic panic to swell up inside of Cassie.

She wasn't tied to the bed and in a desperate attempt to escape she rolled in an effort to move herself off the bed, do anything that would make things more difficult for him.

But before she could make it to the other side of the bed, he rolled her over and straddled her, making it impossible for her to do anything but stare up into his face...her killer's face.

Chapter Fourteen

By the time Mick reached Cobb's Corners he was wild with panic. He'd tried to call Cassie half a dozen times and each call had gone directly to her voice mail.

As he approached the motel, he saw a patrol car parked in the back lot of the fast-food restaurant. Lambert. The name screamed in his head. The restaurant was dark, everyone having gone home long ago. It was a perfect place to park and walk to the motel. He could kill Cassie and then calmly leave the motel and get back into his car with nobody to witness the fact that he'd been there.

The fact that the car was still parked there gave him a little bit of hope. If he'd already killed Cassie he would be on his way back to Black Creek, not lingering here at a crime scene.

Cassie wouldn't have hesitated to open her motel room door knowing that it was the sheriff on the other side of the door. She would have had no reason to suspect him.

Mick didn't have a problem with anyone seeing his presence here. Still, he turned out his lights and drove slowly around the corner to the back of the motel where Cassie's room was located.

He parked several rooms away and got out of the car, closing the door with a faint click. He didn't want Lambert to know he was here. He needed to approach the room with caution. He had no idea what might be happening behind the closed curtains and didn't want to force anything that might result in Cassie's instantaneous death.

Where was Bob Hastings? Why hadn't he seen that something was going down in the room? He'd been assigned to keep an eye on things here. Mick's stomach tightened as he wondered if the FBI agent was dead. Death was the only thing that would keep him from doing his job.

With his gun drawn, Mick approached the window, hoping that there was a slit in the curtains, a spot through which he could see into the room.

He tried to control the tremble of his body as he made it to the glass window by the door.

What he wanted to do was storm the barracks, beat down any obstacle that stood between him and Cassie. Control, he thought. This was the time when a man needed control.

Frustration clutched his throat as he realized there was no way to see into the window, the curtains were all closed tight, not even allowing in a tiny peek.

This close to the door he could hear the sound of a man talking. He leaned his ear against the door, praying that he'd hear Cassie's response.

There was no woman's voice, rather the male voice seemed to be delivering a diatribe of emotion. He frowned. That voice, it didn't belong to Lambert.

"All the blondes, just like her, enjoying the honeymoons that I was supposed to have," the voice said. "It wasn't fair. It wasn't fair that they got to have what they wanted and I didn't."

Perry. Mick was shocked to realize the voice belonged to Alex Perry. He suddenly remembered the brief conversation he'd had with the man in the coffee shop. Perry had told him he'd come close to getting married but it hadn't happened. And it was easy to guess that it had been a petite blonde who had screwed up Perry's wedding plans.

"You have to pay. You all have to pay for her sins." Alex's voice held a kind of stress, a kind of rage that signaled to Mick he was about to snap.

Mick placed his hand on the doorknob and prayed that in all the events that had transpired nobody had relocked the door once Perry had been admitted into the room.

Drawing a deep breath, his gun firm in hand, as a calm resolution swept through him he twisted the knob. He had a single moment to be grateful that it was unlocked before he shoved it open and momentarily froze at the sight of Alex Perry straddling Cassie on the bed.

Perry whirled around and off the bed and with the skill of a ninja kicked out and dislodged the gun from Mick's hand. The gun went flying to the end of the bed as Mick flew toward Perry, undeterred by the lack of a weapon.

Perry had a gun shoved into his waistband, but it was the knife he had in his hand that distracted Mick as he roared like a bull and hit Perry midsection.

The knife slashed, slicing Mick on his arm

as the two men tumbled to the carpeting at the foot of the bed. The white-hot pain of the wound didn't stop Mick. He managed to grasp the wrist of the hand that held the knife and at the same time realized the gun had fallen out of Perry's waistband. There was no way he could grab it and still maintain control of Perry's knife hand, so he kicked it to the side where it couldn't be used against him.

Perry punched him in the jaw, the unexpected uppercut momentarily shooting stars in Mick's vision, but he didn't release his hold of Perry's wrist. He returned Perry's punch, his splitting Perry's mouth as blood slung from the open wound.

He slammed Perry's wrist against the ground in an effort to get him to release the knife. They wrestled and punched as Mick continued to slam his wrist to dislodge his grip on the weapon.

Mick knew this was the most important fight he'd ever have in his life and he fought with every ounce of strength he possessed, but Alex was a worthy adversary.

As Alex delivered another punch to the side of Mick's head and then to his eye, for the first time since the fight had begun Mick feared he wasn't strong enough, he wasn't capable enough to save himself. But worse than that was the fear that he wouldn't be able to save Cassie.

CASSIE WAS INSANE WITH TERROR, not for herself but for Mick. She could only hear the deadly fight taking place at the end of the bed. She couldn't see what was happening. She was afraid to move, knowing there was absolutely nothing she could do to help if she did move. With her hands and ankles bound she was helpless to aid her partner, helpless to assist the man she loved as he fought for their very lives.

She had no idea what had made Mick show up when he had, she couldn't begin to guess what had made him think she needed him. But she prayed he hadn't rushed to her rescue only to lose his own life.

The only sounds audible in the room were the pounding of Cassie's heart and the grunts and smack of fists hitting skin. Who was hitting who? Who was winning the battle?

Sobs choked from her, sobs of terror that she couldn't control no matter how hard she tried. With the duct tape across her mouth the sobs were muffled moans. She cried for him and for herself. This wasn't the way they were meant to die…in a cheap motel room in a little town. They weren't supposed to die because an insane deputy had decided to punish blonde newlyweds.

She frantically tugged at the tape that bound her wrists. If her mouth was free she would have chewed through the tape, but she was stuck with twisting her wrists any way she could in an effort to loosen it.

Somehow she had to do something. Her partner needed her and there was nobody to help him. She worked more frantically in an effort to escape the duct tape.

The sound of a gunshot deafened her. In horror she froze, her heart feeling as if it was about to explode out of her chest. Somebody had been shot. She could smell the scent of blood in the room.

Somebody had just died.

She could smell the scent of death in the room.

It had been Mick's gun that had fired, but had he been in control of it or had Alex managed to get it?

She stared at the foot of the bed, afraid of who might rise up from the floor. Would it be Mick? Or would it be Alex, ready to finish what he had begun?

Her hearing slowly returned and all she could hear was the sound of deep, heavy breathing. Whose breathing? Finally a hand appeared on the foot of the bed and then a second hand and finally Mick rose to his feet.

His jaw was already turning dark and one eye was slightly puffy. Still, he gave her a slightly crooked grin. "And you accuse me of being a mess," he said, his voice cracking on the last couple of words.

He rushed to her side and gently removed the tape from her mouth. Laughter and sobs mingled together as he worked to remove the tape from her wrists.

Once it was free she threw her arms around his neck. "Mick…oh, Mick, I was so scared for you." She gently touched the side of his jaw. "You're hurt."

"A little," he agreed. "But the good news is that the bad guy is dead."

At that moment red spinning lights radiated through the curtains at the window. "Somebody must have heard the shot and called the locals." He went to the door, opened it and immediately put his hands over his head in a gesture of surrender.

As three of Cobb's Corners' finest entered the room, bedlam reigned. One of the officers cut off the tape from Cassie's ankles and helped her to a sitting position on the bed. A female officer went with her into the bathroom so she could freshen up. When she left the bathroom Mick was outside the motel room door being interrogated by a number of men. Apparently Mick made a couple of calls and before too long the room swarmed with FBI agents and Ed Lambert from Black Creek.

Special Agent Bob Hastings had been found under a tree nearby, trussed up like a turkey and unconscious from a blow to the back of his head. He'd been loaded into an ambulance and was being taken to the nearest hospital.

There was chaos everywhere as Cassie found herself telling her story over and over again to various law enforcement officials. She'd been talking for what seemed like forever when she realized Mick was gone.

Sheriff Lambert approached her, his features holding sad regret. "I'm so sorry, Cassie, about what you've been through. I had no idea. I've racked my brain over the last hour trying to figure out if there was a sign I missed, a warning I should have heeded where Alex was concerned, but honestly I can't think of anything."

She touched his hand lightly and smiled.

"Don't beat yourself up too much. None of us saw this coming."

"Agent Tyler is waiting to take you back to Kansas City. Mick has agreed to return to Black Creek and tie up all the loose ends."

She nodded, a hollowness filling up the space where her heart should be. It was over, finished. And there would be no official goodbyes between her and Mick.

Just as well, she told herself a few minutes later as she sat in the passenger seat with Agent Tyler at the wheel. A goodbye between them had been inevitable. It was certainly less painful this way, without having to see his banged-up handsome face, without feeling the desire to fall into the softness of his eyes.

The assignment was over and it was time for her to put it and Mick away and get on with her life. There would be other assignments, although she knew there would never again be a man like Mick. She would never again allow any man as close to her as she'd allowed him.

She slept for most of the ride back to the city and by eleven o'clock the next morning they'd reached their destination and she was taken to meet with Director Forbes.

"Congratulations on a job well done," her boss said as he ushered her into his office.

"Thank you, but most of the congratulations should go to Agent McCane. If he hadn't figured things out when he had, we wouldn't be having this conversation now. I'd be dead."

For the next half an hour they discussed the crimes and he probed her thoughts and emotions to make sure she was psychologically okay. She knew she was fine, other than the ache of her breaking heart.

"Take a week off," he instructed as the brief meeting wound down. "Get your nails done or take a little trip, do whatever you need to do to clear your head of all this. I'll expect to see you back here a week from today."

The last thing Cassie wanted was a week off to think, to reflect, she thought as she got into her car to head to her apartment. The very last thing she wanted was seven whole days to wonder if she'd made a mistake where Mick was concerned.

When she reached her apartment she amped up the air conditioner and immediately went into the bathroom, wanting nothing more than a long hot shower to wash away the feel of Alex Perry straddling her, the sick scent of his madness that she imagined lingered on her skin.

She didn't even unpack her suitcases before heading to that shower. She stood beneath needles of the hottest water she could stand, scrubbing her skin with a bath sponge and vanilla scented shower gel.

She wished it were as easy to wash all thoughts of Mick out of her head as it was to wash all traces of Alex Perry off her skin. She stepped out of the shower and grabbed one of the fluffy towels that awaited on a brass stand nearby.

A place for everything and everything in its place, she thought. No clutter, no chaos…no life. She frowned as she dried off and put on a clean pair of shorts and a button-up short-sleeved tailored blouse.

It took her only a few minutes to unpack, start a load of laundry and then head into the kitchen to make some much-needed coffee.

When the coffee had brewed she poured herself a cup and sank down at the table. The silence surrounded her and screamed with loneliness. Funny, she'd never felt lonely before Mick. He had ushered into her life a kind of loneliness she'd never known before, the kind that asked questions, that whispered regrets, and that called her a fool.

She got up from the table and carried her coffee cup with her into the living room where the throw pillows on the sofa were neatly aligned, the bookcases held paperbacks that were sorted by genre and the two remote controls she used for her television rested side by side on the end table next to the sofa.

A place for everything and everything in its place, but for the first time she felt as if there was no place for her. Where did she fit into this neat, orderly world she'd created?

Stop it, she commanded herself. This was her life, and it had always been fine before. It would be fine again. All she needed was a little time to transition back into it all.

Despite the fact that she knew there was no reason for Mick to contact her, she was vaguely disappointed as the day wore on and he didn't call her. But why should he? she asked herself. He'd held out his heart to her and she'd rejected it, she'd rejected him. Why would he call her now? The assignment was over, loose ends taken care of, and there was nothing left to be said between them.

She went to bed early, exhausted by all the events that had transpired since the time she and Mick had been handed the assignment and Perry's death. Thankfully, she slept without dreams.

The morning sun streaming through the

window awakened her. Normally she jumped right out of bed to start the coffee and get the day going. Today she broke her usual habit. She picked up a paperback book from her nightstand and spent the next hour reading, surprised to discover she felt okay about the break from her usual routine.

She even considered ordering a pizza for breakfast but, realizing she was trying to prove a point to herself, she opted for bacon and eggs instead. Still, just to prove a point she pulled her hair into a messy ponytail and stayed in her pajamas while she ate breakfast, dusted the furniture and listened to the tumble of the clothes dryer.

She knew what she was trying to do. She was trying to force herself to be the kind of woman who would make Mick happy, a woman who could throw away routine, discard any kind of structure and just embrace life as it came.

She would never be that woman, no matter how hard she tried, and she couldn't help but remember that when Glen had broken up with her, he'd told her she was just too screwed up to be loved.

And he'd been a jerk, she told herself as she folded the freshly laundered clothes. He'd been a jerk who hadn't known the finesse of lovemaking, a jerk who hadn't known how to be supportive in any way.

She had just finished folding the last pair of panties when a knock sounded on her door. Instantly, nerves jangled inside her. Nobody ever came to visit her.

A peek out the front window showed her Mick, standing at her door in a pair of frayed denim shorts and a blue-flowered tourist shirt that instantly brought a smile to her lips.

The smile lasted only a moment. What was he doing here? The very sight of him made her heart ache in a way she'd never felt before. As he knocked again she hurried to open the door, wondering if maybe there was some loose end of their assignment that he needed to clear up.

"Nice look," he said when she opened the door to greet him. She suddenly realized she was still clad in her lightweight light pink pajamas.

"I could say the same about you. Hopping on a plane to some tropical island?"

He grinned, and in that gesture Cassie's heart broke all over again. "Can I come in, or are we going to entertain your neighbors?"

"Of course." She flushed with heat and stepped aside to allow him to enter the apartment. She closed the door behind him and watched as he looked around.

She tried not to smell the familiar scent of him that called to her, that made her want to fall into his arms. "What's up?" she asked, pleased that her tone sounded normal rather than radiating with the stress she felt at the moment.

He walked around the living room, obviously taking in her space. "Pretty much the way I imagined it would be." He turned and looked at her, his eyes the welcome green of spring grass. "What I didn't expect was to find you in your pajamas at this time of the day."

Her cheeks warmed with her blush. "It was sort of an experiment." One of his dark brows rose quizzically. "I just decided to do something a little different today and hang out a little longer than usual in my pajamas. You have a problem with that?"

He smiled in obvious amusement. "I don't have a problem with anything about you." His smile fell away and suddenly his eyes smoldered with a dark light she'd never seen there before.

He shoved his hands into his pockets, a muscle jumping in his lower jaw. "Last night was a long night. I've had a lot of time to think. I know you said you didn't want to date when our assignment was over and I don't want you to think I'm some stalker kind of guy, but I can't help but think if you'd just give us a chance you might be surprised."

He pulled his hands from his pockets. "I have to be honest with you, Cassie. You completely take my breath away. I love you more than any other man on the face of this earth will ever love you. You make me want to be a better man. Be my partner, not just at work, but in my life."

There was none of the cocky sureness in him. He looked nervous, almost afraid of what she was going to say. She was afraid of what she was about to say.

In the space of seconds she flashed back to the time she'd spent with him, remembered each and every touch, each and every burst of laughter that they'd shared. Flash forward and she saw herself alone because she'd been too afraid to let down her guard, to trust another human being with her heart, her very soul.

There was no question that her childhood, her parents, had done a number on her, but at what point did she allow them to keep winning? At what point did she let go of the past and allow herself a real life?

"Cassie," he whispered softly. "The moment I saw you on that bed with Alex Perry straddling you I realized I didn't want to live without you. I can live with rules, I can live with structure, but I'm just not sure I can live without you."

Tears sprang to her eyes. "Oh, geez," Mick said helplessly. "I'm sorry. I don't want to make you cry. I shouldn't have come here. It was stupid idea."

"I almost ordered a pizza for breakfast this morning," she said as she swiped at her eyes. Once again he looked at her questioningly. "I wanted to prove to myself that I could break a few rules, ignore my usual routine. It's almost noon and I'm still in my pajamas and the world hasn't come to an end and I don't want to live without you, either. I love you, Mick, and I…"

Whatever she was about to say was stolen away as his lips took hers in a kiss that lit her up from her head to her toes. It was a kiss of such love, of such promise, that she knew this was the man to take her on adventures, this was the man who would finally break down the shell she'd built around herself.

Mick McCane was going to drive her crazy, and she knew she'd probably drive him more than a little crazy, as well. But, they'd laugh together and they'd figure things out. She knew in her heart that he was the man who would love her to death and finally be the home she'd always wanted.

Epilogue

"He's late." Patsy paced the small confines of the ladies' room inside the small church. Her bright blue bridesmaid dress swished around her shapely legs.

"I knew he would be," Cassie replied. "He's always late."

"I'm going to wring his neck when I get hold of him," Lynnette said. "Imagine being late for your own wedding."

Cassie smiled serenely. "Throttling him will officially be my job after today."

"I'm going out front to see if he's here yet." Lynnette left the room.

Eileen, Mick's third sister, reached out to hug Cassie, careful not to crunch the silk-and-lace gown that Mick had helped her pick out. "I can't believe he got so lucky to find you, and I can't believe he was smart enough to grab you up."

"I can't believe I'm so lucky." Cassie turned to look in the mirror and thought about the past six months. Theirs had been a whirlwind romance. Six months of working together, laughing and loving. Two months ago they had moved into a house they'd bought, a nice ranch with a fenced backyard that would make a perfect place for children to play.

They were planning on two children, and Cassie couldn't wait to give Mick a child. A baby would never replace the one that had been lost, but she knew how badly he wanted to be a dad.

She'd learned to relax a bit and he picked up his clothes every morning. She still liked to know the agenda for each day and he still ran late for everything in their lives.

Compromise and communication had been the key to the wonderful, magical love that had blossomed more strongly with each day that passed together.

Cassie couldn't imagine her life without him, and after today she wouldn't have to. She was about to become Mrs. Cassie McCane, and she would have the family she'd always wanted. She adored Mick's sisters and had bonded with them instantly.

She checked her dainty gold watch. The ceremony was supposed to have started five minutes ago. The church pews were filled with coworkers and friends. All that was missing was the groom.

They were leaving in the morning for a honeymoon in Hawaii. Five glorious days of sunshine, beach and Mick. Neither of them had considered the small town in Arkansas as a honeymoon destination.

A shiver of anticipation swept through her at the thought of cold fruity drinks and hot nights with her new husband. There would be surprises…and delays and she would not only survive, but thrive amidst it all.

"He's here," Lynnette said as she reentered. "He's at the altar and they're ready to play the music. Are you ready?"

Cassie nodded, unable to speak for a moment around the lump of happiness that filled her throat. This was it. For the first time in her adult life she was taking a giant leap of faith, and yet felt no fear. Rather, she only felt how right this moment was, how right she and Mick were together.

The three sisters scurried from the room to take their places and Cassie closed her eyes for a moment and centered herself. Mick had offered up a friend to walk her down the aisle, but she'd insisted she wanted to walk it alone.

She was coming to him with no family, and while she couldn't erase her painful past she could move past it. He'd allowed her to see how strong she was and it felt only right that she walked the aisle alone.

She stepped out of the bathroom and took her place, and as the music began to fill the church she started down the aisle. Mick stood at the end next to the minister. His tie was slightly crooked and his boutonniere was pinned on upside down. Chaos…the man was utter chaos, and she loved him with all her being.

As she drew closer, he gave her a smile that threatened to steal all the breath from her body. His eyes were filled with a love she knew would last a lifetime.

When she was halfway to where he stood an impulse struck her, a crazy impulse that under past circumstances she would have never considered.

This time she did. She kicked off her high heels and ran the rest of the way down the aisle, leaping into his embrace as he laughed with surprise.

"I do," she whispered before the minister had a chance to say a word.

"And so do I," he whispered, and then kissed her as the room exploded with hoots and hollers. Cassie knew she had finally come home.

* * * * *